The Greta Garbo Murder Case

The Greta
GARBO
Murder Case

George Baxt

St. Martin's Press   New York

M

Baxt

Feb. 24, 1992

Design by Judith A. Stagnitto

Library of Congress Cataloging-in-Publication Data

Baxt, George.
    The Greta Garbo murder case / George Baxt.
        p.   cm.
    ISBN 0-312-06988-X
    1. Garbo, Greta, 1905—Fiction. I. Title.
PS3552.A8478G74   1992
813'.54—dc20   91-38122
                                                                        CIP

First Edition: March 1992

10 9 8 7 6 5 4 3 2 1

for
Hope Dellon
and
Eleanor Sullivan
with love and gratitude

The Greta Garbo Murder Case

One

She wanted to scream for help, but didn't dare. If someone came to her rescue, how would she explain her situation? Could she dare admit she was spying? Eavesdropping on a conspiracy, or what she and her employer suspected was a conspiracy. Real blood-and-guts stuff, grist for the mills of the dime pulps. She paused in her flight to catch her breath and remove her sandals. It would be easier to run along the sand barefoot. She looked behind her and saw nothing, heard nothing. But still, they could be there, not too far behind, pursuing her, and if they caught her, they'd kill her. They were without mercy, these conspirators. In time of war, mercy is redundant. And the United States was at war, with Nazi Germany and with Japan. Was it only a month since the infamy of Pearl Harbor? God, how time flies when you're in danger.

She climbed a dune and then hunkered down for a moment to gain her bearings. Under the Pacific blackout it was almost impossible to see anything. Only the stars were twinkling, as only the stars over Santa Monica could twinkle. There was a curtain of haze over the moon, and the waves breaking against the shore sounded like the staccato of gunfire.

Garbo. What the hell does Garbo have to do with this? While eavesdropping in the tastelessly furnished mansion just a few hundred yards past Marion Davies's immense beach house, she'd heard Garbo's name mentioned several times.

"Garbo would be perfect." A man's deep baritone, German accent. Although with the war on, nowadays for German you could read Swiss or Austrian.

"Isn't she a bit old?" Woman's voice, continental, but which brand of continental? Hard to detect.

"Is thirty-seven so old?" Pleasant voice. European too, but what part European? France? Hungary? He repeated his question. *'Is* thirty-seven so old?"

"I don't give a good god damn how old she is, we *need* her." The deep baritone, very officious. Undoubtedly used to giving orders and demanding and receiving respect.

"Why not Dietrich?" The woman, continental voice.

A derisive snort was followed by the baritone's, "You think Garbo's too old? Dietrich's forty-three, God bless her."

"Oh, she can't be. She's so divine looking." A new country heard from. Possibly Italy, British educated. Male.

"I want Garbo." The baritone nailed his demand to their ears.

"Hush." The woman, continental voice. "I think someone's out there."

The woman held her breath. She had managed to raise the window slightly without their hearing her. What had she done to give herself away? Oh Christ, it was a poodle. A nasty black poodle with ribbons in its elegant, expensive coiffure. It wagged its tail and licked her face while she gave it a rough shove away from her. Roundly insulted, the dog gave voice, and, fearful of discovery, the woman took off. Luckily, the dog didn't pursue her. But she heard a door open and a voice shout, "There! Over there! Heading toward the dunes! I see something!"

"Here! See! The window is slightly open. Someone's been listening."

"Stop shouting! Quiet! You'll wake up William Randolph Hearst."

"It's about time someone did." Possibly Italy, British educated.

"Wh-wh-wh-what the hell's g-g-going on out there?" Marion Davies was a vision of middle-aged dissipation, standing in the enclosed garden of her Santa Monica beach house, one hand on her left hip and the other holding a fresh highball.

"I don't hear anything," said her melancholy guest, her voice smoky and husky and reeking with despair.

"I w-w-wonder who's living in that b-b-b-big dump."

"I only hear the crashing of the waves." Her chuckle was dry and brittle. "Better to hear the crashing of waves then the crashing of careers. No, Marion?"

"Y-y-y-yes Greta."

"Marion, why is it you never stuttered on screen?"

"S-s-s-self c-c-control. Have another sherry."

"I still have some."

"Have more. We're up to our hips in amontillado. The old bugger knew there'd be a war so he had gallons of it imported from Spain or wherever it comes from."

"You're not stuttering."

"It comes and it goes."

"You're a fraud."

Davies smiled. She admired her guest's unique beauty. William Daniels, the cameraman, had said of her, "Greta Garbo doesn't have an unphotographable angle. You can place the camera anywhere and she'll emerge on film more breathtaking than an old master."

"Why didn't you marry John Gilbert?" Davies asked Garbo.

"He wanted children."

"So?"

"Somewhere there's an unborn child who's terribly lucky I'm not its mother."

"What a terrible thing to say about yourself."

"Why haven't you had children?"

"Out of wedlock? Are you mad?"

Garbo's laugh was like an explosion of dynamite. "All these decades living in sin . . . ha ha ha . . . and you wouldn't consider mothering a bastard?"

"I *am* mothering a bastard. He's asleep upstairs. What are you staring at?"

"Worms."

"What kind of worms?"

"Insignificant ones, I'm sure. Without a care in the world. They don't face a meeting with Louis B. Mayer tomorrow morning."

"You still under contract to Metro?"

"On paper, yes. In my soul, no."

"You haven't done a picture in a year. I thought *Two-Faced Woman* was kind of cute."

Garbo got up from her chair and stretched her arms lavishly. "There were two great cataclysms in 1941, Pearl Harbor and *Two-Faced Woman*. She leaned over and resumed staring at the worms. "Marion?"

"Yes, dear."

"I wonder how worms make love." Davies suppressed a shudder and swigged her highball. "Don't you suppose they repulse each other? And yet, there are so many worms, billions and trillions of them. I should imagine, come to think of it, worms must be very sexy."

"Greta, if you ever decide to go into analysis, can I sit in on a few sessions?"

Garbo now concentrated on the haze-covered moon. "Look at the moon."

"I've already seen it."

"Look at the haze. They call that a Bomber's Moon."

"Is that a fact?"

"Yes it is. It is perfect for raiding airplanes. Not too bright to give them away, not too dull to obscure their targets."

"Where the hell do you pick up stuff like that?"

"The *Reader's Digest,*" came the world-weary reply. "I think I'll go home."

"Why, for crying out loud? It's early yet."

"I must be up early to run on the beach."

"What an exhausting idea. You Swedes beat hell. No wonder there's such a high rate of suicide in Sweden."

"Thank you for dinner, it was lovely."

"Oh?" asked Davies through an alcoholic haze, "Did we eat dinner?"

Fifteen minutes later, Garbo sat alone on her patio facing the ocean, deep in thought. As she did too frequently, she dwelt morbidly on the past. Her abusive, alcoholic father. Her passive and permissive mother. Then she thought of Marie Curie and wondered why Louis B. Mayer was no longer interested in filming Curie's life story.

"Nothing happens!" Mayer had insisted at their last meeting. "She discovers radium. Big deal!"

"But you made *two* pictures about Thomas Edison."

"They both lost money!" Mayer puffed ferociously on his cigar. "For a while there I considered your doing something really different, like playing Mother Goddam in *The Shanghai Gesture.* Y'know, Von Sternberg's bomb. But then I figured, what the hell, you've played enough whores. Even though a Chinese whore would've been a change of pace." He smiled benignly. "So I didn't bother you with the idea."

"Thank you for having the good taste to spare me your bad taste."

And tomorrow morning there was to be another confrontation with the despised head of Metro-Goldwyn-Mayer. I am thirty-seven years old, she thought, and I am still a beautiful woman. I am very wealthy, I need never want for the rest of my life. This tiresome war, how long could it possibly last? A year, maybe two, and then I could resume traveling. The Far East, how I yearn to travel to the Far East. Damn the Japanese. Damn the Germans. Damn Louis B. Mayer.

"Who's there?"

She heard a noise coming from beneath the patio. She looked over the railing, and saw what seemed to be the figure of a woman emerging from behind a rose bush and running across the sand toward Peter Lorre's house. She thought of alerting the police and just as quickly scrubbed the idea. The house swarming with police was not her idea of absolute privacy. Probably some young girl playing hide-and-seek with her lover.

Lover. How long has it been since I've had a lover? And if I had one now, how would I handle the situation? My career teetering on the edge of oblivion, a world at war and I'm not cut out to be a soldier. I could be a leader, but never a follower. What shall I do? What shall I do? She snapped her fingers. I'll make some Ovaltine.

Peter Lorre was urbane enough to smile charmingly at his unwelcome guest.

She had scrabbled at his back door and for a moment he thought it might be a neighbor's dog come to beg for scraps. On the other hand, it could be the police. He hastily secreted his stash of cocaine in its hiding place in the butler's larder when the scrabbling became more insistent. He crossed to the back door and opened it a crack. "Yes, what do you want? Don't you know there's a blackout?"

She pleaded, "Please let me in. I've lost my way. I need to call a cab."

It was a young voice and young voices usually emitted from young faces and young faces usually belonged to young bodies and Lorre was partial to young bodies. "Hurry." He pulled the door back and she hurried in. She was carrying a purse and a pair of sandals, and the windblown hair partially obscuring her face could not camouflage her beauty.

"Thank you, you're very kind." Then she recognized him. "You're Peter Lorre."

"Yes," he acknowledged eagerly, "and my wife's away."

"If you could show me the phone."

He wanted to show her something else, but Jack Warner had only recently cautioned him about his indiscretions with young women. "I'd be delighted to show you my phone. I think you'll find it quite attractive. It's lilac, the only lilac-colored telephone in all Hollywood." She followed him into the tastefully furnished sitting room with what was usually a spectacular view of the Pacific Ocean, but now was heavily draped to keep the light in and the view out. "You look all tuckered. Has someone been chasing you?"

"I'm not sure. I think so. I was walking on the beach. . . ."

"That's very dangerous in the blackout. . . ."

"I do it frequently. Nothing untoward has ever happened."

You've never met Lorre before, he was thinking, and then silently admonished himself. He said, "You were walking on the beach, and . . . ?"

"I suddenly heard these noises behind me, you know, that slop-slop noise shoes make when they're running on sand."

"Oh yes. I'm a slop-slop *maven*."

"Maven?"

"Connoisseur, Yiddish version." His real name was Laszlo Lowenstein.

"Maven," she repeated solemnly. "I like it."

"Shall we go back to the slop-slop noise?"

"If you insist. Well anyway, I began to run. I just panicked. I ran past Marion Davies's place. . . ."

"Why didn't you ask for help there?"

"I couldn't find the back door."

"Marion is always misplacing things."

"And then I hid behind a rose bush under a patio. . . ."

"That sounds like Greta's place."

"Garbo?"

"Hardly Rabinowitz."

"I should have liked to have met Greta Garbo."

"Well, apparently you've shaken your pursuers." There was a firm knock at the back door. "Apparently you haven't." He indicated a door to her left. "The only person who looks in that closet is my wife. Closets are her secret vice and on indiscreet occasions my undoing." The knock was now firmer.

"Perhaps it's your wife."

"Goodness no. She has a key. She even knows how to use it." She slipped into the closet as he went to the back door. He opened it and recognized one of the private policemen the community had hired to patrol the area since war had been declared.

"Why, Thomas Toth, I do declare. What brings you to my back door at this hour?"

"Have you seen a young woman?"

"If I had, I wouldn't tell you."

"That's usually Groucho's line."

"What kind of a young woman did you have in mind?"

"One on the run. She was last seen by Miss Garbo's neighbor darting around under her patio."

"Anyone would be safe under Greta's patio."

"Obviously you haven't seen her."

"Obviously. Is this my cue to invite you in for a drink?"

"No, thanks. My partner's waiting for me near your dune."

"It's a very comfortable dune. I designed it myself."

"Mr. Lorre, you sure are a caution." He disappeared into the darkness and Lorre shut the door, hoping the light from the kitchen hadn't attracted any Japanese bombers cavorting overhead in wild abandon. He hurried back to the living room and opened the closet door. She wasn't there.

"Hello?" He shut the door and crossed to the adjoining library. She wasn't there either. He went from room to room, but there was no sign of his night visitor. He said aloud, "She doesn't exist. It was all my imagination. I better go easy on the cocaine."

At ten o'clock the following morning, Greta Garbo sat across from Louis B. Mayer. His good right arm and master spy, Ida Koverman, sat near Mayer. Garbo wondered if Koverman's perpetual smile had been plastered onto her face.

"Now Greta darling," Mayer said cozily, "we certainly wish to continue making pictures with you, but you have to understand, they can't carry big budgets anymore." Garbo said nothing. A sphinx never speaks. "Your major market is lost to us." He was uncomfortable. "Europe is gone. You're big in Europe, very big, but you've lost your American audience. But darling, we'd like to continue starring you and we'll stockpile these films and when the war is over, we'll bombard Europe with them."

She finally spoke, mournfully. "Poor Europe. Always bombarded."

"You agree, don't you, Ida?"

"Oh yes," piped Koverman, who had years ago mastered the Hollywood art of saying yes.

"So you see, Greta, we can't spend too much money on your next films. We have to bring them in on the budgets we have for the Andy Hardy and the Doctor Kildare series."

"I see."

"But we can do some very lovely subjects. We have an idea for one where you play twin sisters. . . ."

She moaned, "But I just played sisters and it was a disaster."

"But they weren't really sisters," interjected Koverman, "it was a woman making believe she was her own twin sister. . . ."

"Please Ida, don't remind me."

Mayer stepped in swiftly. "These twin sisters are very different. One is a schoolteacher in Brooklyn and the other is a Nazi spy. And the schoolteacher is mistaken for the Nazi and she's in trouble with Conrad Veidt. . . ."

"It is not for Greta Garbo, Louis."

Mayer rubbed his eyes. "We have a play by Noel Coward, *We Were Dancing*. Norma Shearer wants to do it, but I think I can talk her out of it."

"Please don't. I hear she's having a hard time with Mickey Rooney."

"That's a lie!" roared Mayer.

"Oh Louis, I don't care if she is or she isn't. Noël Coward is very droll. I am not droll. I am sad."

"Well, I'll tell you. Jack Warner has a movie coming up called *The Conspirators*. All-star cast. Of course you'll get top billing. He asked for Hedy but I know if I tell him you're interested, he'll be beside himself."

"You wish to loan me out to Jack Warner?"

Mayer spread out his hands. "Why not?"

Garbo said forlornly, "Louis, I don't want to be a loan."

$\mathcal{T}wo$

Later that day, sharing the patio with her closest friend and confidante, Salka Viertel, Garbo asked mournfully, "What's to become of me now that I'm forgotten and forsaken?"

Salka smiled as she applied a match to a cigarette. "You'll never be forgotten and you'll never be forsaken." A Polish refugee, the woman had struggled her way to Hollywood and in no time learned English and became one of the film industry's highest paid scriptwriters. She had worked on several of Garbo's films and was one of the few people to win the star's trust and admiration.

"Mayer wanted me to be Andy Hardy or Doctor Kildare."

"How dare he!" Salka's indignation smouldered, waiting to erupt. She loathed Louis B. Mayer.

Garbo smiled. "Not really. He just wanted me to make very inexpensive films." She folded her arms across her chest and contemplated the beautiful sky. "So after all these years, I am no longer an MGM star."

Salka's eyes widened. "He canceled your contract?"

"By mutual consent. Divorce is always the best when it is useless to continue a dying marriage."

"Ha! Every studio in town will be after you now!"

Garbo's housekeeper, Lottie Lynton, stepped onto the patio and asked, "Shall I do tea, Miss Garbo?"

"Oh yes," said Garbo enthusiastically, "let's have tea! You would love tea, wouldn't you, Salka?"

The writer said dryly, "Why, I'd kill for some."

Garbo said to the housekeeper, "With some biscuits, chocolate-covered ones. And maybe some of those funny little finger sandwiches you make with cucumbers and radishes. Would that be too much trouble on such a beautiful day?"

"No trouble at all, ma'am." She retreated, not happy at having overheard Garbo was no longer with Metro. She knew her employer was rich but she also knew she suffered from wanderlust. But still, with a war on, where was there for her to go except possibly Yosemite National Park and she couldn't quite imagine Garbo hiking trails and frightening the animals.

"I have never played a nun. Mayer wanted me to do *The White Sister* years ago but I said no, Lillian Gish had already done it beautifully as a silent. So Helen Hayes played the nun."

Salka recognized the preamble to what would be some startling revelation.

"Perhaps I should become a nun."

"In what order?"

Garbo ignored the mockery staining her friend's voice. "In no particular order."

"You could never be a nun." Salka blew a smoke ring and then left her wicker chair to join Garbo on the wicker couch. She took her friend's hand and held it gently. "Now look, darling, you're still much too young to continue sequestering yourself."

"I feel that God needs me."

"I don't know if you've noticed, but God has been very tiresome lately. Though even He must know that somebody needs you. Get out into the world."

"The world is at war. Ah! I could be a nurse! You remember how I nursed people in *The Painted Veil.*"

"*That* stinker."

"But Salka, it was one of your babies! You helped write it."

"It's one of my babies that should have been stillborn. Now stop being so fey and start being practical."

"I am practical, which is why I am so lonely."

"You brought that on yourself. Now's the time to come out of your shell and join the war effort."

"I could be a very good soldier. I'm a very good shot. Shall I enlist?"

"Greta, I wish you'd hang a FOR RENT sign on cloud nine and come down to earth."

Garbo was on her feet and pacing restlessly. "It's no good, Salka. I can't do bond tours the way Carole Lombard and Dorothy Lamour do because crowds terrify me. I can't visit hospitals and cheer up the wounded and the dying because the wounded and the dying make me ill. I wouldn't know what to say to them. I can't dance with the boys at the Hollywood Canteen because I'm not a good dancer."

"You're a marvelous dancer."

"Clark didn't think so."

"That cluck. What does he know?"

"Do you think it would be difficult to get to Switzerland?"

"What the hell do you want with Switzerland?"

"It's neutral. I'd be safe there."

"You're safe here, for crying out loud."

"No I'm not. Last night there was a prowler."

"Really?"

"It was a woman. She was under my patio, behind the rose bush."

"I see. You were over at Marion's, drinking again."

"It was only sherry. A presumptuous amontillado. Why do rich people buy cheap wines?"

"Why do rich people drink them?" Her sly thrust didn't escape the actress. "Did you report your prowler?"

"Of course not. The police would have invaded my privacy."

"If there *was* a prowler, you could have been robbed or even killed."

"There most certainly was a prowler." They recognized Peter Lorre's distinct voice immediately. Both smiled. They adored him. Just about everyone in the industry liked the pixieish actor with his wicked sense of humor. He came up from the beach and chose a perch on the wooden railing that protected the patio. "It was a woman. A very pretty woman." He told them about his encounter the previous night.

"And she disappeared into thin air?" Garbo's hand was at her throat, a moment borrowed from one of her silent films, *A Woman of Affairs*.

"Poof!" said Lorre. "Mr. Saloman reported her."

"Saloman? The old man next door?" Saloman's house was situated between Garbo's and the Marion Davies beach house. His was becomingly modest, as became a retired insurance man.

"He happened to be opening a window to let some air in when he saw her under your patio. It seems she'd been hiding behind your rose bush."

"You see, Salka!" Her eyes sparkled victoriously. "I was not hallucinating!"

"I didn't say you were hallucinating."

"You didn't have to say it, but you implied it. Thank you, Peter, thank you. I might have been incarcerated in a lunatic asylum."

"I hope that never happens," said Lorre, "you'd drive them crazy."

"What's in that envelope you're carrying?"

"A script."

"Have you read it?"

"Yes."

"Is it a good script?"

"It's a very good script."

Lottie Lynton arrived with the tea wagon and three cups and saucers, having heard Lorre's entrance. "Shall I pour, Miss Garbo?"

"No, thank you, Lottie. We'll look after ourselves." The housekeeper withdrew and Salka Viertel took command of the tea service. She wrinkled her nose at the plate of dainty sandwiches, preferring heartier repasts just as any good Pole would. "So, little Peter, what is the script about?"

"The Maid of Lorraine."

"Joan? Joan of Arc?"

"The kid herself."

Garbo said, "But who would care to see Joan of Arc portrayed on the screen today? I mean hers was such a teeny tiny war compared to today's Armageddon."

Salka interjected, "She's one of the great symbols of freedom. I happen to think she was a rustic nincompoop who pulled off one of the greatest con acts in history. Even so, more power to her. After all, they nominated her for sainthood and she won the poll by a landslide."

Garbo now stood tall and majestic, her hands crossed on her bosom. "I shall be a saint."

Lorre smiled as he lit a cigarette. "You'd be a most imposing saint."

"I really mean it, Peter. I too can be a martyr."

"I brought this script for you to read."

"Lemon, Peter?" asked Salka.

"It is not. The script is very good."

"I meant in your tea, dear. Lemon or milk?"

He chose milk, wondering why the rich never offer cream.

"Why do you want me to read the script? Ah, yes! There's a good part in it for you and you want my opinion. I am so flattered."

"Listen, Greta, cut the Peter Pan act and let me talk some sense into your head."

"Bravo, Peter, have one of these odious little sandwiches."

Peter dismissed Salka with an abrupt wave of his hand. "Greta, you would be magnificent as Joan of Arc."

"I'm too old."

"Crap. You can play anything you want."

"I can't play Ginger Rogers."

She was offered no argument. Lorre said, "Ginger couldn't play Joan of Arc."

Salka snorted and said, "Try telling *her* that."

"Still, I'm too old. Joan was a frisky young colt. A very foolish and self-willed creature who succeeded because she dealt with people who were dumber then she was. I mean, take the Dauphin of France. . . ."

"I have," said Lorre after sipping his tea and finding it tepid and distasteful. "I'm playing the part."

"Really? But you're much too old."

Lorre said to Salka, "She's a broken record, this afternoon. Too old, too old, too old. Sarah Bernhardt triumphed as Hamlet when she was sixty and wore a wooden leg!"

"Still, she was much too old." She selected a chocolate-covered biscuit. "I suppose with a good cameraman, say, William Daniels, I could . . ." The rest of the sentence drifted out to sea, caught in the surf, on its way west. Salka winked at Lorre. They knew Garbo was hooked.

Greta curled up on the wicker couch nibbling at the chocolate biscuit like a well-brought-up mouse. "Which studio is producing?"

"It's an independent."

"Oh please, Peter, I have read all about these independents proliferating out here. They always run out of money."

"This one could never run out of money. The producer and backer is Albert Guiss."

Salka whistled. Garbo's mouth formed a moue. Then she said, "What did *Life* magazine call him? The international figure of mystery."

"His money's no mystery," said Lorre. "The film's budget is five million dollars."

"Don't be ridiculous," scoffed Garbo. "You could make five lavish productions with that kind of money. Why *Gone With the Wind* cost about a third of that to produce!"

Said Salka, "Without even reading the script I can tell you one million would be more than enough to put Joan on film. Possibly more if they really want Greta. She doesn't work for lunch money."

"They're offering Greta one million dollars," said Lorre.

It was Garbo's turn to whistle. "That's obscene."

Lorre shrugged. "It's the kind of obscenity I wouldn't mind indulging in."

"Albert Guiss." Coming from Garbo, the name sounded Wagnerian. "Have you met him?"

"Oh, yes. He has a fabulous connection for getting me cocaine."

"Oh, Peter," Garbo groaned, "someday this addiction will kill you."

"Don't be ridiculous. It's just a pleasant habit. Everybody in the industry knows I use it."

"It will be your downfall."

He laughed. "Bela Lugosi uses more than I do, and he never stops working."

Salka advised him, "Bela's an even bigger fool then you are. Look at what he's sunk to doing. Poverty Row horror films for a fraction of the salary he could be earning."

"I've got big news for you. Just this week Universal Pictures put Bela back under contract at his original money. Thanks to the war, horror thrillers are back. *Dracula, Frankenstein, The Wolf Man.* They tried to get me but Jack Warner wouldn't sell them my contract, bless his dreadful hide."

"But he's letting you do this one for Guiss," said Salka.

"Nobody says no to Albert Guiss."

"Is there a director signed?" asked Garbo.

Lorre set his cup and saucer down and waved away Salka's offer of a refill. "An old friend of yours."

"Oh yes? Who?"

"Erich."

She thought for a moment, and then her eyes widened, like Pandora opening the box. "Von Stroheim?"

"You're joking." Salka was genuinely astounded.

"It's his chance for a big comeback."

Greta stroked her chin, deep in thought, and then said, "No wonder it has a five-million-dollar budget. Erich will spend every penny of it."

"He will make a brilliant film."

Garbo nodded. "Yes. That is possible. Erich can be very brilliant. Even his failures are larded with his special genius. He will act in it too?"

"No. He's strictly behind the camera, that was a firm stipulation by Guiss."

"Good for Guiss. Score one for him. What's the shooting schedule?"

"Three months."

"There are many battle scenes?"

"A great many."

"Three months, then, will not be long enough for von Stroheim. He'll need six months. And you know what a stickler he is for realism!" She was back to pacing the length and breadth of the patio. "He will demand real corpses! Ha ha ha!" Salka laughed too, but Garbo wasn't kidding. She knew the reputation of the arrogant and profligate von Stroheim. "There will be real blood spilled. No tomato soup for von Stroheim unless it's piping hot for his dinner. Ha ha ha!" Then she paused and her hand flew to her throat. "And my God! When Joan burns at the stake . . . !"

"Stop that, Greta," cried Salka, upset. "He wouldn't dare burn you at the stake. He'll need you for retakes."

"There's a wonderful bunch lined up for the Inquisitors." Lorre had regained their attention.

"Boris Karloff's playing the chief inquisitor."

"Oh good, good, that is very good." Salka nodded her approval as Garbo continued to speak. "The industry has never given him a chance to show what a truly fine actor he really is. Who else?"

"Jean Hersholt."

"Also good. We were together in *Susan Lenox*. He's good to work with. He isn't selfish. He gives."

"Victor Jory."

"Another one misused by the industry. It's all very impressive. Still . . ."

Lorre said gravely, "Greta, sit on your doubts."

She continued pacing in silence. Then she placed her hands on the wooden rail and gazed out at the Pacific Ocean. Her face illuminated nothing but its breathtaking beauty. She saw dolphins cavorting, but her eyes reflected nothing. It was a replica of her final moment in *Queen Christina* when she stood at the ship's railing after the death of her lover, feeling nothing, hearing nothing, saying nothing, her mind and her face a blank. Finally she spoke. "I will read the script."

"Read it several times," implored Lorre.

"I will read it and I will think about it. You don't realize, Peter, but in my seventeen years in films, I only worked for one studio, for Louis B. and Metro." Her eyes misted. "It was my home. They looked after me. They catered to my every whim. I was a daughter there such as I never was to my own father and mother. But now I have been banished, I'm an orphan. I must choose my next set of parents with great care and discrimination." She looked away from the sea to Peter Lorre. "I don't know if I want Albert Guiss for a father. I really don't need a mother". She smiled warmly at Viertel. "Salka is a good mother. My good mother." She crossed to the older woman and placed her hands on her shoulders. Then abruptly she withdrew her hands and resumed pacing. "They talk about refugees and displaced persons. They whisper about concentration camps. Look at me! I'm a refugee! I'm displaced!" She made a sweeping gesture with her hand. "And this is my concentration camp!"

Lorre commented wryly, "At least you've got hot and cold running water."

"Don't mock me."

"Don't mock yourself. Enough of these self-indulgent dramatics and read the script."

"I'll read it tonight after my lonely dinner."

"I'll join you for dinner if you like," the actor offered.

"I prefer to be lonely. Are you going, Salka?"

"I've got to get back to the script I'm working on." She crossed to Garbo and kissed her lightly on the cheek. "Phone me when you've finished reading the script. Come on, Peter."

When they were out of Garbo's earshot, Lorre asked Salka, "What do you think? Do you think she'll do it?"

"Joan's a challenge for her. And you know Greta."

"Does anyone know Greta?"

"A few of us do. She dotes on challenges. And don't believe that crap about being orphaned by Metro. She loathes the place. She's delighted to be free. She dreaded the thought of doing another film for them. Now then, what about this woman last night?"

"Well, it was the strangest thing." He warmed up to the subject. "She was quite beautiful, and I have a suspicion she was European. Her English was unaccented, but it had that lovely lilt foreigners have when they learned their English in England. You know, like me."

"By you that's a lovely lilt?"

"Don't be unkind."

"How old was this woman?"

"Her early twenties at the most. But she was genuinely frightened. Marion Davies thinks she has something to do with that ugly mansion adjoining Marion's estate."

"Who lives there?" asked Salka.

"That's it. Apparently nobody. At least no one's been seen entering or leaving it since the Wolheims moved out so hastily last November."

"Oh yes. The Wolheims. A strange family. If they were a family."

"You knew them?"

"Only by sight. Greta and I saw them a few times when we walked on the beach. Father, mother, three sons and a daughter. At least that's what we assumed they were, father, mother, sons and a daughter. Yet none of them resembled each other."

"Perhaps the children were adopted."

"Peter, you think of everything." They arrived at her car in Garbo's driveway. "Tell me, dear. How did you get to Albert Guiss?"

"Albert Guiss got to me."

"Really, how so?"

"He sent a man named Werner Lieb to see me; he and a woman named Risa Barron are to be the actual producers of the film. Guiss will act as executive producer. Lieb is quite a charmer. I think he's German originally but he said he was educated in Italy and England. His is another of those weird accents I can't place. Me, you know I'm from Germany. You, I know you're from Poland. But this fresh breed of refugees pouring into the country, they're such hybrids. I mean even Guiss is hard to place. But that deep baritone of his. When he speaks, the room trembles. I think even his whisper could shatter glass."

"Why Joan of Arc?" asked Salka. "Why something so dark and heavy? Greta's proven in *Ninotchka* she can play comedy, why not something light and graceful co-starring with Cary Grant or Fred MacMurray? That's what Greta really needs in a vehicle at this stage of her career. Peter, she's at a dangerous crossroads and she's well aware of it. Greta's no fool. She has no delusions about herself. She's a complete realist despite the misinterpretations about her."

"Werner Lieb put it to me this way and you'll have a few surprises when you read the script."

"Oh yes?"

"Oh yes. Lieb says what Guiss has in mind is an inspiring and very patriotic film. This Joan is very fresh and sassy. She even tells saucy jokes."

"Does she die laughing?"

"This is an inspirational Joan. No long-winded speeches about hearing voices. She's a very democratic young lady out to do battle against the oppressors of her time. I find the script delightful, and I haven't found many delightful scripts lately."

"I can't wait for Greta's reaction." Salka got behind the wheel of her car. "I suppose the Dauphin's part is a very meaty one."

"Oh it's delicious. I get to do many wicked things."

"Who wrote this masterpiece?"

"Something named Gustav Henkel. A very pleasant fellow."

"Henkel. Sounds German to me."

"I thought so too, but when I asked him, he said he was Hungarian."

"You can't trust Hungarians."

"Actually, the script does need work. I suggested they get Bertolt Brecht to do a polish on it."

"Henkel didn't object at the suggestion of another writer being brought in?"

"Quite the contrary. He seemed quite affable about it."

"He can't be a real Hungarian. They are mostly objectionable."

"Why are you so hard on Hungarians?"

"One of them stole my virginity." She started the motor, while Lorre refrained from commenting, Petty larceny.

Greta Garbo, from her living room window, had been watching Salka and Lorre deep in conversation. Lottie Lynton entered and asked, "Is there something I can get you? I've cleared away the tea things."

Garbo said huskily, "I wish I could read lips."

Three

Chief Inspector Herbert Villon of the Los Angeles Police Department was awaiting the visitor the desk sergeant had just announced. He was reading Louella Parsons' gossip column in the Hearst newspaper and frowning. Lolly, as Louella was known to the industry, was taking Greta Garbo severely to task for not contributing to the war effort. Lolly's rival and archenemy, Hedda Hopper, had beaten her into print that morning by announcing in the riveting prose usually attributed to illiterates that Queen Garbo had been dethroned by the powerful Louis B. Mayer and was now just another unemployed actress. Hedda was a personal toady of Mayer's, and he gleefully fed her the tidbit of Garbo's defection.

Mayer had said to her over the phone, "Make it read like no other studio is interested in her."

"That won't be easy, Louis," said Hedda while examining her reflection in a hand mirror and reappraising a millinery horror positioned atop her head. "Your son-in-law wants her for an adaptation of Robert Hichens's *The Paradine Case.*"

"That *momser* is doing it just to annoy me. With all the eligible men in Hollywood my daughter had to choose to marry David O. Selznick. *O* for *Oy vay*."

"Warner wants her for *The Conspirators*."

"Too late, I gave them Hedy and it's a firm deal."

"Herb Yates at Republic is prepared to offer her *Lady from Louisiana* opposite John Wayne."

"Fat chance she'll do that. He'll end up with Ona Munson or some other half-baked *shlepper*."

"Funny," said Hopper as she laid the hand mirror on her desk, "I can't imagine Metro without Garbo. It's like an opera without arias."

"I know, I know. But she wouldn't compromise. She wouldn't take a cut in salary. She wouldn't settle for smaller-budget films. That Swedish bitch called my bluff! But just you wait. She'll see what it's like working for those other bums. She'll come crawling back."

"My money's on Greta."

Mayer exploded. "I thought you were my friend!"

"I am, Louis, I am. But Greta's always commanded my respect. She was always kind to me when I was down and almost out."

"Didn't I keep you eating with small parts? Didn't I?"

"Yes, Louis, yes, as you constantly remind me."

"Be a good girl, now. Let her have it with both barrels."

"Yes, Louis."

What emerged from Hopper's typewriter was a tad more merciful then Mayer demanded, yet it was still painful to read. But Parsons let go with a full salvo, forgetting that Garbo was one of Marion Davies's personal favorites, and Davies was her boss's mistress. Later, when both Hearst and Davies admonished her severely, Parsons took the reprimands bravely, which didn't prevent her from taking occasional potshots at Garbo in the future.

Chief Inspector Villon threw the newspaper in the wastepaper basket as his visitor knocked lightly on his door.

"Come on in!" shouted Villon.

The man who entered was tall, blond and thirtyish, with a strong face. His smile was almost shy and boyish. He shut the door and crossed to Villon, who had stood up to greet him, with his hand extended. "Arnold Lake, sorry I'm late."

"Sit down, Arnold." They both sat. "When'd you get in?"

"After lunch. The train was six hours late. We kept being shunted onto sidelines to let troop trains go through. They warned me when I left D.C. the trip would be no picnic."

"Couldn't you hitchhike a ride on an army plane?"

"The brass don't like that. Everybody's overheated with spy fever. You're not a spy, are you?"

"No, I'm just a movie-struck cop. Did you read Louella Parsons today?"

"No, I use her paper to wrap up my garbage."

"She attacked Greta Garbo." It sounded more infamous than the attack on Pearl Harbor.

"Why don't you punch her in the mouth?" asked Arnold.

"I couldn't hit a woman." Then he recognized he was being kidded. He laughed. "You know, living here in L.A., born here, brought up on the movies, it's like everyone in the industry is an old buddy of mine, whether I've met them or not. And I go back to the silents. But Garbo. You don't attack Garbo. She's an icon. A goddess. A living legend." He paused. "I must sound like a movie-struck kid."

"You sound very refreshing. Anyway, shall we get down to it?" He spread a dossier on the desk. "My credentials." Villon gave them a cursory examination.

"Fine. So they sent you here to lock horns with Albert Guiss."

"I always get the fun assignments."

"Have they any proof he's working for the Germans?"

"None whatsoever, only a scintilla of a suspicion. I just had a quickie sandwich with one of my associates. You'll get to meet her eventually."

"Pretty?"

"Very?"

"Can't wait."

"I thought you were married."

"It ended due to artistic differences."

"Anyway, my associate has been tailing a woman named Risa Barron, who's very close to Guiss."

"How close is close?"

"Mistress close."

"That's close."

"Last night, she followed her to a house on the beach at Santa Monica. She managed to overhear a plot to do something that might involve your goddess."

"Garbo?" Villon almost hit high C. "Garbo involved with spies?"

"They're trying to get Garbo involved. And we don't know if they're spies or not. There was a lot of palaver about Joan of Arc and they must have Garbo. . . ."

Villon leaned back in his swivel chair. "That's movie talk, Arnold. That's not spy stuff."

"Don't be too quick to dismiss it. The personnel at that meeting were exclusively heavy with foreign accents."

"So's every other movie coming out of the studios these days."

"The meeting was conducted by Albert Guiss."

"In person?" Villon straightened up.

"It wasn't a reasonable facsimile. And why conduct a business meeting under cover of darkness in an uninhabited beach house?"

"Can you beat that? Cloak-and-dagger stuff right under my nose. But listen, Guiss is known to be a perfectly normal eccentric."

"That's an oxymoron."

"I don't care what kind of a moron it is. Guiss has been under suspicion as a Nazi sympathizer from almost the inception of the movement," Arnold explained, "But nobody's been able to get the goods on him. He operates through dozens of phony setups and organizations. We think he has a brilliant operation going through which he launders monies into fifth-column hands. We're positive he was Franco's angel in Spain but we can't get the goods on him."

"And America has welcomed him with open arms."

"Why not? He has billions invested here. Does the thought give you a chill that he's probably silent-partnered in any number of defense industries?"

"It'll take months for my spine to thaw." They were silent for a few seconds. Then Villon continued, "So now he's going into the movies."

"That's right. But we can't figure out why. This movie he's involved in is about Joan of Arc."

"Joan of Arc? Aw, come on now. Ingrid Bergman's more right for that than Garbo."

"I don't think so."

"Come on, Arnold. Ingrid's younger than Garbo, she's much more right for it."

"I thought you were a fan of Garbo's."

"Oh until death do us part, but much as I love her, one has to be realistic about casting her. She's just too damn old for the part."

"Anyway, why argue? Bergman's under contract to Selznick and she's hot as a pistol and he'll never lend her to an independent."

"Don't kid yourself. He's short of cash, I hear, and . . ."

Arnold Lake held up his hands. "What are we arguing about? Who gives a damn who plays Joan? They can give it to Hattie McDaniel for all I care. I'm here to nail Guiss if he needs nailing."

Villon wiped his forehead with a handkerchief. "I get so heated up about casting. It's more fun than homicide. Okay, Arnold, so I'm to provide you with a cover. That's no problem. You're here on a special assignment working with me. What about your girl?"

"They almost caught her snooping last night. She managed to pry open a window, the better to hear them, but someone wised up to it and gave chase. She eventually ended up in Peter Lorre's place seeking refuge."

Villon melted in front of Arnold Lake's eyes. "Peter Lorre. My hero. Did you see him in his first American movie, *Mad Love?*" Without waiting for an answer, he was on his feet mimicking Lorre. " 'I, a poor peasant who have conquered science,' " his simulation of Lorre's voice was uncanny, " 'Why can't I conquer love?' "

"Bravo," said Arnold softly, wondering if some men wearing white coats were waiting in the corridor.

"I do impersonations occasionally," said Villon with a slight tinge of red in his cheeks. "So Peter Lorre rescued her."

"Well, not quite. When Lorre was occupied elsewhere, she high-tailed it out of his place. You see, she suddenly realized that not only was Garbo's name being noised about at the secret meeting, there was much ado about Peter Lorre."

Villon's chin dropped. "Peter Lorre a spy?"

"Why not?" countered Arnold with a sly smile. "It's perfect casting."

Garbo walked alone along the beach, a large floppy hat pulled down over her head until the brim obscured her face, her body wrapped in a grey oilskin windbreaker. Seagulls flapped overhead, squawking at her intrusion, and in the distance, a foghorn sent out mournful, depressing signals. If anyone else was about, she was oblivious to his presence, so deeply absorbed was she in her private thoughts.

Joan of Arc.

Peter Lorre.

Albert Guiss.

Erich von Stroheim.

Louis B. Mayer.

Salka Viertel.

Quite an impressive assemblage. Of not much box-office value on a movie theater marquee, but with the addition of Greta Garbo, it at least bespoke quality.

I am thirty-seven years old. I own a huge area of this seafront. I own large parcels of land on Rodeo Drive in Beverly Hills. I own an estate in Sweden, an apartment in New York. Ha, apartment *houses* in New York. I own my house here on the beach. I have furs and jewels and stocks and bonds and equities and my health, why shouldn't I retire from films? Why should I do Joan of Arc? She was probably a lesbian, and there's enough innuendo in my life about lesbianism. But still, can I retire with that dreadful *Two-Faced Woman* as the final film by which I'm to be remembered? Have they forgotten my *Camille,* my *Ninotchka,* my *Anna Karenina?* Some say it is tragic I have never been given an Academy Award, but so what? Luise Rainer won two years in succession, and now no one will hire her—Louis B. Mayer saw to that when she left Metro. And now he seeks to poison me the same way with the help of the gossip columns. Poor Hedda. Louis cracks the whip and Hedda jumps. Poor Lolly, with her uncontrollable bladder and alcoholic husband, who is she to cast the first stone, or even the second stone, or any stone at all?

The sigh she sighed was heavy enough to topple a wall. She took the hat off and stood still, like a lighthouse offering guidance to lost ships, but there were no ships in sight. It was after six in the evening, almost two hours since she'd been with Salka and Peter Lorre, and the curtain of darkness had descended. There were the moon and the stars to guide her back to her house, but where were the moon and the stars to guide her into the future?

In Peter Lorre's house, the grandfather clock in the downstairs foyer chimed six o'clock. Behind the bar, the actor poured himself a large scotch and water. He guarded his whisky supply zealously now that liquor was in short supply. He crossed the room to his favorite chair, intending to reread the script of *Joan the Magnificent* (as it had recently been retitled), when the doorbell rang. He muttered an oath, placed his drink on an end table and went to the front door. The door was covered with a heavy black drape to conform with the blackout law. He moved the drape aside a bit and then opened the door a crack. He recognized an old friend wearing a black trilby hat and a black velvet cape, presumably designed by a vampire.

"Bela," said Lorre, "how nice of you to drop by." Pleasant, but insincere.

"Good evening, Peter," said Bela Lugosi in his well-oiled Hungarian accent. "I have come to throw myself on your mercy."

"Come in. Quickly."

Once inside, Lorre guided Lugosi to the living room where Lorre's drink awaited him. As he followed in Lorre's wake, Lugosi said with a sweet smile, "Is it possible I could borrow a cup of cocaine?"

Lorre froze in his tracks. "A cup? That's a half year's supply!"

"Cup is merely a metaphor for my distress. I've been away on location and in my absence, my supplier was found floating in the ocean off the pier in Venice, a section of clothesline around his neck. Apparently he displeased someone who lacked a sense of humor. My supplier was a very funny man." He was referring to the Venice community just north of Santa Monica, a hotbed of male body builders who occupied an area dubbed Muscle Beach.

"Have a seat, Bela. Would you like a drink?"

"Some red wine?"

"Of course." Lorre went to the bar for the drink. "I'm a bit low on my cocaine supply. The war, you know, it makes importing a bit difficult."

"Yes, I'm well aware. The federals have quadrupled their guard of the Mexican border. Of course, one could always arrange to take a trip down there and bring a good quantity back, but that's a risky business."

"Especially so when you're foreign born. If you're caught, you get a fine and a jail sentence. This is followed by deportation, and this is hardly the time to be parcel-posted back to Hungary."

"No time is the time to be sent back to my native land." He took the wine from Lorre and sipped. The lascivious look of pleasure on his face had Lorre expecting to hear in the distance the plaintive howling of wolves, Dracula's Children of the Night. "Delicious. But then, you have always been a connoisseur. But what is this?" He'd espied the *Joan the Magnificent* script.

Lorre told him about the upcoming production. "They want Garbo to play Joan."

"Garbo?" Lugosi drew out her name like he was pulling at some chewing gum. "I was with her in *Ninotchka*. A very charming recluse." He thought for a moment. "She's too old to play Joan. They need someone younger, like Jane Withers." He heard Lorre choking on his drink. "Are you all right?" Lorre sat down, gasping for breath. "Is there something in it for me?"

"As a matter of fact there might be. The part of the jailer. It isn't big, but it's showy."

"It would be nice to be part of a prestige production again. I'm back at Universal."

"I heard. Congratulations."

Lugosi shrugged. "It's a living. I'll never die a rich man, but still, I can keep up the mortgage payments. . . ."

". . . And the cocaine payments. . . ."

Lugosi shrugged again. "There are no wars or dropped options in my cocaine dreams. Will you be able to help me out, even a soupçon?"

"I'll help you, of course. Do you know Erich von Stroheim?"

"Not terribly well. Why?"

"He's going to direct the film. You'll need his approval."

"Why shouldn't he approve me?"

"Erich is a very strange man. He is pursued by a unique set of grotesque private ghosts. Hard luck favors him."

"How can you say that when he is signed to direct this million-dollar extravaganza?"

"The gods tease him. On one hand, they reward him lavishly, and with the other hand, they doom him to bankruptcy. I hope this works for him. We'll see. I'll get the cocaine." He left Lugosi alone. Lugosi picked up the script and began to read. He chuckled. Then he laughed. Then he roared. "My, my, I didn't know Joan of Lorraine could be such a scream. I suppose for more than one reason she was the toast of the town."

Greta Garbo was reading the script. As usual, first she frowned, then she uttered a *huh,* then she turned a page and smiled, then she said a quick *ha,* and, to no one in particular because she was alone in the room, she said, "They don't need me, they need Fanny Brice." Pause. "She's also too old."

Four

Erich, how good to see you again." Greta's hands were outstretched to him and he took them while bathing in the warmth of her affectionate greeting. "It has been too many years."

"Not since *As You Desire Me,*" he reminded her.

"Oh my yes. And Hedda was my sister-in-law in that one!" They shared a laugh, seeming to have forgotten that von Stroheim had arrived with Gustav Henkel, the author of the script. Lottie Lynton was hovering in the background waiting for instructions from Garbo. Garbo acknowledged Henkel. "And who is this?"

"Good heavens, Gustav, forgive me. On the few occasions that I see the great Garbo, she strikes me with awe and leaves me with amnesia."

"Erich, you're too kind." She took Henkel by the hand and led the undistinguished-looking young man into the living room. "You are Gustav Henkel and a very fine writer."

He said in an undistinguished voice, "You are too kind."

"Not at all. I'm grateful for having read a fairly decent script at last."

Von Stroheim stiffened. "Only 'fairly decent'?"

Lottie Lynton trembled. She sensed a hidden danger in the man.

Garbo smiled at von Stroheim. "It's not as though Mr. Henkel has written the Bible."

Von Stroheim scoffed. "What would you know about the Bible? I'm sure you've never read it."

"Not all of it. Just the racy parts. Ha ha ha. Lottie, see what our guests would like. Drinks? Tea? Something to eat?" Wine was requested and Lottie went to work. "So, Erich." They took the seats she indicated. "You think this script is perfect?"

"Of course not, Greta. Gustav acknowledges it needs work."

Gustav spoke. "Oh yes, it does need work. The problem is, I don't know exactly what kind of work it needs. You see, this is my first attempt at writing a screenplay."

"So? Well then it's quite good for a first attempt. If a bit giddy. I mean, I don't quite see Joan playing craps with her jailers. I don't even think craps existed in those days."

Henkel smiled, dazzling them with a display of what looked like Roquefort cheese. "I worked very hard for the irreverence. I think we take our saints too seriously. I mean, before being elected to their eminence, they were quite ordinary people. I think if most of them were alive today, they'd be bemused by all the fuss."

"If they were alive today," said Garbo somberly, "we wouldn't need them." She waited while Lottie served the drinks and returned to the kitchen. "Well Erich, this is quite an undertaking. Five million dollars. Almost enough to rebuild Dresden."

"Not quite, but still a generous, staggering sum. Albert Guiss wants this to be his monument, much as *Birth of a Nation* is Mr. Griffith's."

"You like this Mr. Guiss?"

"So far I haven't found anything to dislike."

"So much has been written about him, all so arcane, so enigmatic, so like . . . like . . . ah! Orson's *Citizen Kane!* Why are we always fascinated by men like Albert Guiss? Mr. Henkel, how well do you know Albert Guiss?"

Henkel stared into his Chardonnay, but there was nothing written there to prompt him. "He has been very kind to me."

"He paid you well for the script?" Then hastily, "I take that back. It's none of my business."

"I got a very decent sum, for a beginner."

Von Stroheim took center stage. "Tell me what bothers you about the script, Greta."

She sipped her Bordeaux, set the glass on the coffee table, crossed her legs, and fixed her gaze on the director. "The construction needs improvement. Joan is lost for at least ten pages midway into the script and that's much too much. Not because it is the star part, but because what takes place while she's offscreen is hardly very interesting. Who cares what her family thinks about her taking command of the army? It is enough to see Joan leading them into battle. Families don't care about successful children, only about the sums of money they can send home."

"I see. That's valid. Henkel?"

"What? Oh yes. Valid. Very valid. Families are boring."

There is something unreal about this little man, thought Garbo. Little men. Henkel, a small man. Von Stroheim, a small man. Lorre, a small man. She heard von Stroheim ask, "What else, Greta?"

"Much of the dialogue is terribly amusing. In fact, Mr. Henkel, a few times I laughed out loud, and for me that is very rare." She cleared her throat. "But too often the jokes are unnecessary. I mean, if you are looking to do a farce about Joan of Arc, then Joan must be played by someone like Martha Raye."

Henkel smiled. Garbo didn't notice it. How had she guessed he adored Martha Raye?

"On the nose," said von Stroheim. "There's an overabundance of levity."

Garbo leaned forward, fingering the string of pearls around her neck. "Erich, shouldn't we consider restoring her being burned at the stake?"

"If we did, wouldn't you be disturbed by my paranoia for realism?"

"Only the critics dare burn Garbo." She cocked her head to one side. "Think about it, Erich. If it's truly unnecessary, then we'll do without it. Falconetti was so magnificent in her version, but then, it was silent, wasn't it?"

"And excruciatingly slow and boring. My Joan shall move at a steady pace," von Stroheim said, underlining his statement with a machine-gun—fire snapping of his fingers, "zip, zip, zip, so the audience won't have a moment to let their minds wander. You must understand, Greta, that we cannot undertake any revisions until you are firmly committed to the project. By that I mean your name on a contract, signed and sealed."

"Of course, of course."

"Have you discussed this with your agent?"

"I have dismissed my agent. I suspect he was allied with Louis B. Mayer in the recent unpleasantness. I am my own agent." Von Stroheim flashed a "heaven help us" look at Henkel. Garbo was known as a shrewd trader who could drive a very hard bargain. "Peter Lorre says Guiss will offer me a million dollars."

"Yes, that is so."

"Mayer says my only value is in the European market. But there is no European market. So where will Mr. Guiss recoup his investment? Or doesn't he care, he's so wealthy."

"He cares. He's a businessman. But in this instance, he is more of a patriot. He feels Joan is a valid symbol of the struggle against oppressors, in this case, the Axis villains." Garbo saw Henkel's eyes blinking wildly, like semaphores running amok.

Garbo said, "I find it hard to envision Albert Guiss wrapped in a flag of patriotism. Surely the man is a country unto himself."

Henkel said hotly, "Mr. Guiss is a great patriot. A very great patriot. He is a very great man."

"Cool it, Henkel," cautioned von Stroheim. "What about us, Greta?"

Her eyes widened, puzzled. "What about us?"

"Will we get along?"

"How will I know until we start working together?"

Von Stroheim smiled. "And you call Guiss enigmatic. Are you joining us?"

"I'm inclined to. But I have to discuss this with someone."

"But Peter Lorre told me Salka Viertel urges you to do this project."

"Yes, she does. But there's someone else. An old and trusted friend who is also psychic."

He threw up his hands. *"Ach!* Psychic! I hate that word!"

Henkel said in his copyrighted nondescript way, "I'm sure you'll be interested in meeting Albert Guiss. I know he's a very great fan of yours."

"For an investment of five million dollars, he should be!" She said it with good humor, and Henkel did something with his face that she suspected might be a smile. She was glad he hadn't parted his lips. She dreaded the sight of those awful teeth. If she did the film, she would insist his teeth be capped or removed.

Peter Lorre entered from the patio. "Am I interrupting?"

Von Stroheim was glad to see him. "Peter! Help me convince Greta to be our Joan."

Lorre looked at Garbo as though she were a naughty little girl.

"But of course you must do the film!" He sat on the couch next to Garbo. "There are so many of our refugee friends down on their luck who'll be put to work." Garbo couldn't bring to mind any names; all the refugees she'd met in Hollywood seemed to be doing quite well, especially the untalented ones. Lorre said to von Stroheim, "Haven't you told her Hanns Eisler is to compose the score?" His eyes pounced on Henkel. "And we will ask Bertolt Brecht to improve the scenario. And for supporting roles in addition to those I mentioned to you yesterday, Greta, there will be Fritz Kortner, Alexander Granach," he ticked off the names on his fingers, "Hertha Thiele, Albert Basserman, his wife Elsa . . . oh so many more. We literally need a cast of hundreds, don't we, Erich?"

"It's a tremendous cast."

"I'm overwhelmed," said Garbo.

Von Stroheim said to Lorre, "Greta is afraid our Joan is a little too frivolous."

Garbo clapped her hands. "Listen. I have had a thought about Joan as to how I might play her, but I was afraid you might find it, well, a bit outrageous."

Von Stroheim said staunchly, "But I love outrageous. *I* am outrageous. Tell me, tell me quickly, how do you think you might play her?"

Garbo stood up, towering like Gulliver over three Lilliputians. "I think it is quite possible that Joan was really a man." Lorre bit his lip. Von Stroheim felt the blood leaving his face. "A transvestite!" Henkel was wearing his awful smile and Garbo turned her back on him with revulsion. "What if I was to play the part androgynously?"

Von Stroheim finally found his voice—it was a rare occasion when he lost it, even briefly. "Greta, we have to think of the Catholic Legion of Decency. Those watchdogs of American morals are very strict and very dangerous. If they refuse us a seal it will cost us hundreds of thousands of dollars in lost attendance."

"I see." She stroked her chin. She had a solution and shared it. "They couldn't stop me from thinking I'm androgynous, could they?"

"No they couldn't," said von Stroheim.

"Well then, that will be our secret. If I play it."

"If if if!" raged Lorre. "Of course you'll play it!"

"Peter, don't push me." They heard the danger in her voice, and Lorre mustered his familiar pixie grin.

He said, "It's just that we're all so anxious to get going."

"I know. I know. But don't burden me with your anxiety. I've just rid myself of one albatross around my neck. I have to think twice before trying another one for size."

Von Stroheim stepped in swiftly. "This is not an albatross, Greta. This will be a milestone in film history. Your Joan will be exalted!"

"Even by *The New York Times?*" Her eyes twinkled.

Von Stroheim put his hands on her shoulders. "In *As You Desire Me,* we acted together. Ever since, I have wanted to direct you in something. In my exile in France, I thought of trying to talk Gaumont into letting me direct you in *Madame Bovary.*"

"Ah! Why didn't you?"

"I was too late. They were already doing it. But now, Greta, now, with Joan of Arc, here is the opportunity for my dream to come true. Greta, make my dream come true. I will never have an opportunity like this again."

"Yes you will. If I do it and it's a success, they'll be knocking down barriers to get to you. Tomorrow, Erich. Tomorrow. You will have my answer tomorrow."

Von Stroheim persisted, "You will never have an offer as magnificent as this one."

She cocked her head, as she usually did when amused. "Oh no? Supposing I tell you I already have received a very magnificent offer, although it was several years ago."

Hands on hips with exasperation, Lorre asked, "And what was that?"

"Adolf Hitler asked me to marry him." They were stunned. "Didn't you know I'm one of his three favorite stars? He sent the offer through the German ambassador here in Los Angeles. Of course I refused. I had already lived in Germany back in 1925. It was awful. Do you know who his other two favorites are?" She paused for effect and then told them, "Marlene . . . and Minnie Mouse. Ha ha ha ha ha!"

"You took a foolish chance last night," said the young man whose name was Martin Gruber. He and his companion sat in the booth of a coffee shop in the Culver City section of Los Angeles, just a few streets away from the imposing MGM studios that bordered Washington Boulevard.

"I was doing my job," said Lisa Schmidt. "How did you find out about it?"

"Guiss was discussing it on the phone this morning."

"And you guessed that the woman was me?"

"I don't know anyone as rash and headstrong as you. I wouldn't try it again."

"Why did they use the house?"

"It's the only property of Guiss's the FBI hasn't bugged. They don't know he owns it."

"They do now."

Gruber chuckled. "He'll find someplace else. He's really marvelous."

"Does Guiss trust you?" asked Lisa.

"Of course not. He trusts nobody."

"Not even Risa Barron?"

"Hardly Risa Barron. She's ambitious. She wants power. I gather he enjoys her in bed. So he makes her the film's co-producer. It's only a title."

"And a fat fee," said Lisa flatly.

"Guiss is very big with fat fees. He can afford to be. He has billions."

"Who *is* Guiss?" Lisa asked.

"Who is he? He's his own invention. And he astonishes and frightens an awful lot of people."

"Doesn't he frighten you?"

"Sometimes. He doesn't seem to notice me very much. I'm an employee and as such I have my uses. I'm unobtrusive. I don't ask questions other than what pertains to my work. I like working for him." Lisa was looking at her wristwatch. "Are you in a rush?"

"In a while. I'll have a spot more of coffee."

"A pressing appointment?"

"As a matter of fact, yes. It's for a job."

"But you have a job," said Gruber.

"I have time for another." The waitress he had signaled refilled her cup. "If I can get it, my boss wants me to take this job."

"What doing?"

"It's work on a film going into production soon." Gruber suspected Lisa was playing with him, and she was.

"Doing what?"

"Assistant to the director."

"And the name of the film?"

"Joan the Magnificent." She sipped her coffee, her eyes meeting his over the rim of her cup.

"You're insane."

"No more insane than you as Guiss's personal secretary."

"Lisa, please. Don't do it. Get out of this. Last night you were lucky. The blackout was on your side. But this new madness . . ."

"Martin, my darling, I can look after myself. And just think, if I get the job, I will not only be working with the mad Erich von

Stroheim, I will get to meet the magnificent Garbo. Luck is on my side, Martin. I feel it. I know it. Cheer up, Martin. This is all a magnificent adventure, the opportunity of a lifetime."

He added gravely, "Of a very short lifetime."

She sipped her coffee and looked away from him. A very short lifetime. He was possibly right.

Five

Small people, thought Garbo, suddenly I am surrounded by small people. She sat across from the diminutive yet exotic Mercedes de Acosta, Cuban born, now a Hollywood scenarist, and once, briefly, her lover. Mercedes's tastefully furnished apartment was in a new highrise on Doheny off Sunset Boulevard, and it afforded a magnificent view of Hollywood. It was ten in the morning and they were drinking strong coffee weakened by strong cream.

"How's for an onion roll and cream cheese?"

Garbo shook her head No. "Why do I have such a presentiment about this picture? I am so uneasy. It's as though heavy heavy hangs over my head. And yet, the more I think about it, the more I am compelled to undertake Joan."

"You're too old for it, but then, you were too old for *Camille* and you were brilliant."

"Too old, too old. Ah me, soon I will be at an age where there will be very little available for me to play. In three years I'll be forty. What will I do then?"

"In three years there may not be a world existing, so take hold of the present and with both hands. What you need is a lover."

"Oh God no." Garbo's voice was so powerful a chandelier shook. "I have my hands full coping with myself."

"What about Guiss? Have you met him yet?"

"No, but I have made discreet inquiries. There are those who find him above suspicion. And there are others who consider him beneath contempt. Why should I care about Guiss? He's the financing, I'm the artist. I am so torn. It hurts me so to feel that Hollywood is turning its back on me."

Mercedes snorted. "Why do you give a damn? Hollywood is only a state of mind where insincerity is an art."

"I will have no friends."

"You can always buy new ones."

"That's cruel."

"That's Hollywood. Do the movie."

Garbo brightened. She needed to hear the woman's support. She respected de Acosta, who had a quick mind and remarkable taste and a unique talent for friendship. She wrote well too, but had yet to equal Salka Viertel's success. Salka and de Acosta had a guarded friendship, colored by their possessiveness toward Garbo. Garbo was the important thing they had in common. They worshipped her, they treasured her, their lives were all the better for knowing her.

Garbo was happy, and when she was happy she looked a decade younger. "You really want me to do it? You really do?"

"Absolutely. Think, Greta. You'll be working. You'll have a reason to eagerly greet the morning, to get up and go to the studio and reign like the queen you are. Believe me, my beloved Greta, you'll never be equaled. You will be the legend they will speak of in cathedral tones."

"Could I become a saint?" Garbo's hands were clasped as she watched an inquisitive pigeon make a three-point landing on the balcony.

"Why not?"

Garbo smiled. "There's a pigeon on your balcony. Do you suppose it has brought a message?"

"It's brought filth is what it's brought. Shoo, you filthy thing," Mercedes cried as she clickety-clacked onto the balcony in a pair of absurd shoes in which she could barely maintain her balance. The pigeon stared at her in defiance for a few seconds, then flew to the railing and, with a haughty toss of its head, soared off in search of hospitality elsewhere.

The doorbell rang, and Garbo was annoyed. "You didn't tell me you were expecting anyone else."

"I'm not. It might be the concierge with the mail. He usually brings it up himself. Now stop fretting and pour yourself some more coffee. It's pretty damned good this morning if I must say so myself." She opened the door. "Alysia!"

"You're surprised? Did you forget you invited me for coffee?"

"Oh my God. Forgive me! It completely went out of my head. Greta needed some advice on a script and . . ."

"I could come back later, if you like." The woman was in her forties and her clothes would have been stylish a few years earlier. She nervously clutched a threadbare handbag and her shoes were badly in need of repair. Her accent, Garbo decided, was definitely German, and her voice was brimming with sadness and disappointment. Garbo was on her feet and said generously:

"Mercedes! Bring your friend inside. There's plenty of coffee for all of us."

Mercedes smiled the smile that had enchanted so many lovers. "Come in, Alysia. Greta's in a sunny mood. Let's make the most of it. It's an historical moment." The woman followed Mercedes into the living room, where Garbo stood with a warm smile decorating her lips.

Oh good, thought Garbo, she's as tall as I am. This could be a sign, a reversal of my fortunes. "Hello," said Garbo, "I'm Greta," as though the woman needed to be reminded.

Mercedes took over. "Greta, Alysia Hoffman is an old friend of mine."

Garbo gasped. "Alysia Hoffman! But of course! How stupid of me not to recognize you! We were in *Gösta Berling's Saga* together in Sweden!"

Hoffman laughed. "You remember! Oh how wonderful!" She said

to Mercedes, "Mine was such a small role I'm flattered Greta remembers me. And Mauritz Stiller, who directed, was so good to us all."

At the mention of Stiller's name, Garbo's face darkened. Mercedes saw the change at once and asked, "What's wrong?"

Garbo swiftly smiled again. "Oh, nothing. I still get sad when I hear Stiller's name. Even though he's now dead over a decade, I still remember how badly he was treated here." She said to Alysia, "When Metro wanted him back in 1925, he wouldn't sign the contract unless they took me too." She sat, and Alysia sat across from her. Mercedes brought a cup and saucer for the new arrival, and the three became cozy around the coffee table. "He was so brave and so foolish, we were both so broke, we couldn't pay our hotel bill." She laughed. "But after many delays, *Gösta* finally opened, and at last Stiller got the acclaim he deserved. And Louis B. Mayer, wouldn't you know, was in Berlin at the time and made him an offer. But Stiller loved me. . . ."

"I thought he was a homosexual," interrupted Alysia.

"But not seriously. He only dabbled in it. You know, the way you occasionally dip into a collection of essays. Mauritz loved me and only me. He wanted to marry me. I was so innocent and so *fat."* The three laughed. "I really was, how do you say, *zaftig.* When Mayer finally agreed to take me, I had to agree to lose fifteen pounds. I lost twenty. When I got to Hollywood and saw how Stiller was being mistreated, I lost my appetite. I became an insomniac. I tried to fall asleep by counting producers." She looked past the two women, out the window, past the balcony, into the blue beyond where memories were surfacing from a long dormant suppression. "Then I met Yonnie."

"John Gilbert," Mercedes interpreted for Alysia.

"Oh well, that's all water under the bridge. So tell me, Alysia, how long have you been here in America?" Garbo was genuinely interested.

Alysia placed her cup and saucer on the table. "I came in through Mexico. That was over half a year ago. It wasn't easy, but a friend had a friend who was very influential, and I finally got my visa."

A friend had a friend who was very influential, thought Garbo, and was disturbed that her mind had conjured up Albert Guiss. "And are you acting?" Just as quickly as she asked the question, she regretted it. She could see the poor woman was enduring sorry straits.

"I'm trying to act. I've had two bit parts, but two bit parts can hardly sustain a career. It's not easy, after having graduated to leading roles in Germany. I played opposite Connie Veidt, Jannings, Werner Krauss."

Garbo said quickly, "Don't mention Connie's name in the same breath as the other two. They're Nazis."

Alysia spread her hands and said softly, "To me, it is more important that they are artists. Anyway, now I do part-time work. I sit for babies, I help a seamstress—thank God my mother taught me how to sew. Do you have anything that needs repairing? I could give you a special price."

Garbo was embarrassed. Having known poverty in her youth, she didn't care to deal with the poverty of others. She said, surprisingly enough, "We must try and find you something in my new movie."

Mercedes smiled. That was it. She must phone Salka and Peter Lorre. Garbo positively will play Joan.

Alysia Hoffman's eyes were misting. "What is your new movie?"

Mercedes swung into action. When enthusiastic she was a dynamo. In less than three minutes, Alysia Hoffman heard about the movie, the director, and who would probably be in it, and Alysia was enthralled.

Alysia said to Garbo, "Perhaps I could be your stand-in. We're the same height, we have similar coloring. . . ."

"Wouldn't you rather be in front of the camera?" asked an astonished Garbo.

The woman replied pragmatically, "A stand-in works through the time it takes to shoot the film. A part," she said wistfully, "that could be a matter of perhaps a few weeks, or even a few days."

Garbo thundered, "This is von Stroheim directing. The film will take an eternity. We shall watch each other growing older under his despotic direction." She laughed. "Every day we'll examine each other's faces for fresh wrinkles. My frown marks shall deepen into ditches and I shall develop an ulcer."

"Charming," said Mercedes dryly. "That attitude won't get you very far."

"Don't worry about me, Mercedes," said Garbo, "you should understand my strange sense of humor by now. After all, even though I'm a Swede, don't they call me The Melancholy Dame? Not very funny, is it. Well, go to it, Mercedes."

"Go to what?"

"To the phone and dial Salka and Peter Lorre and probably von Stroheim, and you hadn't forgotten you had invited Alysia for coffee this morning, as she was needed to underline the sadness of the refugee actor. . . ."

"Don't be cruel, Greta," snapped Mercedes.

"I am not being cruel. I'm glad my mind is made up." She rose to go. "Alysia, you will soon be working in the studio. I promise you that, although I'm sure the promise was made by someone else in line ahead of me."

The woman stood up. "I'm sorry. I didn't mean to offend you."

"But I'm not offended at all. I think it's very funny—ha ha ha. Now I must go and immerse myself in Joan of Arc." She marched to the door. She opened the door and then faced Alysia with a smile that was almost beatific. "Really, I'm delighted my mind was made up for me. Now I have a purpose for the next six or seven months." And this was followed by a heavy sigh. "But oh God! What do I do after that?" She slammed the door shut behind her.

Alysia Hoffman said, "Isn't she amazing?"

Mercedes replied, "She likes to think so. Well Alysia, that was a lovely performance on your part. What would you have done if she had offered to bring you an armload of dresses for repairing?"

"Repaired them. I really *can* sew. You wouldn't have an onion roll in the kitchen, by any chance?"

A few hours later, Herbert Villon and Arnold Lake were lunching in a Chinese restaurant with Lisa Schmidt. Lake couldn't take his eyes off the woman, he found her beauty so breathtaking. He found the courage to ask, "Why didn't you try acting?"

"What . . . and starve to death?" She watched Villon shoveling moo goo gai pan into his mouth with a pair of chopsticks. "You know, Arnold, you asked me that very same question over a year ago when I first joined the department."

"I don't remember."

"Understandable. You were so drunk. It was in your apartment, about ten minutes before you tried to rape me."

"I didn't!"

She smiled at Villon. "He did. But I made it easy for him, he was so adorable."

"I still am," said Arnold.

Villon had stopped eating and now drank of Lisa's beauty. "A cutie like you shouldn't take such chances."

"Live dangerously, that was my father's motto. He was a high-wire walker with the circus."

"And now the daughter walks the high wires," said Villon, "figuratively speaking."

Arnold asked Lisa, "When do you start work for von Stroheim?"

"Tomorrow, you'll be happy to know."

"Whether they've got Garbo or not?"

"Von . . ." She smiled. "He asked me to call him that when he patted my knee. Von. Anyway, Von is positive she's going to do it. All the big guns are aimed at her and this morning she was getting an opinion from her friend Mercedes de Acosta, who has been primed to convince her to do the film. What's bothering you, Arnold?"

"I think Miss Garbo is about to be in very grave danger," said Arnold. Villon dropped the toothpick he'd been using to excavate between his teeth. "They're too anxious to get her, and only her."

"She's a very big name," said Lisa, "even if her last movie was a dud. The picture stands to make a fortune in Europe once the war ends. Albert Guiss can certainly afford to wait to recoup his investment."

Arnold asked, "Can you trust Guiss's secretary?"

"Trust Martin? As much as you can trust any paid informant. Martin has the morals of an alley cat. He's apparently very good at his job or Guiss wouldn't have him. It's the first time he's had a male secretary. Before Martin, they were always women."

"What made Guiss switch?" asked Villon.

"From what Martin could gather, a couple of them sold information to magazines and newspapers, and I know one had a fling with him and then died during the abortion. Anyway, Martin's been with him several years now and let's be grateful . . . ," she smiled coquettishly, ". . . that he also appreciates my beauty."

"Be careful he doesn't cross you," warned Arnold.

"Let him try. I'll separate him from his privates. Anyone for tea, gentlemen?"

Samuel Goldwyn's studios were in the heart of Hollywood on Santa Monica Boulevard, and Goldwyn was happy to rent space to independent producers. It was here that *Joan the Magnificent* would be shooting. Goldwyn had rented them space on a three-month lease with monthly renewals.

In his well-appointed office, Goldwyn said to his faithful assistant, Sophie Gang, "You better believe me, Sophie, this lease with Albert Guiss is going to be an annuity. He has to have a shoe loose in his head to let von Stroheim direct."

"Von better not get wind of how you feel about him. He can become very nasty."

"Oh yes? If I hear he said something off-color about me I'll sue him for defecation of character. You better believe me, I'll swear that on a stack of bubbles. Now let's get back to business. What's next on the magenta?"

Sophie's eyes crossed and then just as quickly uncrossed. "Gary Cooper isn't crazy about playing Lou Gehrig."

"Goddammit!" roared Goldwyn. "That Gary is becoming a milestone around my neck!" He pushed his chair back from the desk and crossed to the window. He drank of his kingdom and once again felt content. "Thank God I own this studio lox stocks and barren. It's my Garden of Eden, Sophie. My paradox."

The *Joan the Magnificent* company occupied a large suite of offices on the Goldwyn lot. In Erich von Stroheim's freshly painted, redecorated and refurnished office, the director was pacing the room attacking the air with a riding crop. He wore magnificently tailored jodhpurs and a brown turtleneck sweater that made him look even shorter than he was. Greta Garbo sat in an easy chair, wearing beautifully tailored navy blue slacks, a pink blouse and a beret arranged devilishly on her head. Lisa Schmidt, soberly dressed in a skirt and blouse, with her hair pulled back and kept in place with a blue barrette, sat in a chair next to von Stroheim's oversized desk and took notes.

"Noted and agreed," dictated von Stroheim, "Miss Garbo is to have Adrian design her one outfit required for the role of Joan."

Garbo formed a bridge with her fingers. "Why aren't the producers here?"

"They aren't necessary. They're just figureheads. *I, von Stroheim,*" he said, beating the air mercilessly with the riding crop, "am the real producer of this epic. Now what else?"

"There's an actress named Alysia Hoffman. I want her for my stand-in."

Von Stroheim stopped in his tracks. "I usually choose the stand-ins."

Garbo said firmly, her chin rigid, "I want her."

Von Stroheim asked sternly, "Is she the right height? Is her coloring favorable?"

"Yes and yes." Garbo snapped each word. She could see Lisa Schmidt was relishing this test of wills. Two Olympians locked in combat; she was delighted.

"Have her come in and see me. Miss Schmidt," he barked her name, "set an interview with this Alysia Hoffman."

"You may set the interview, because you certainly should meet her, but I won't appear on the set if she is not my stand-in."

"Miss Garbo! You have signed a contract!"

Miss Garbo, thought Lisa, not Greta? We *are* annoyed.

"Miss Garbo wants Miss Hoffman. And if Miss Garbo doesn't have Miss Hoffman," she said, shifting in her chair for emphasis, "Miss Garbo shall be taken severely ill and confined to her home."

She raised her voice. "It doesn't matter a damn who's my stand-in."

"It most certainly matters to me! Everything in my productions must be perfection!"

"I have no use for perfectionists. They never accomplish anything, they're so preoccupied with being perfect. Oh let's get on to other matters. I've been invited to dine with Guiss tonight and I'm not looking forward to being on exhibition."

"You are his star. You owe him the courtesy of dining with him."

"Wealthy people make me uncomfortable. I'm sure he's a megalomaniac, a monomaniac and a Seventh-Day Adventist." She propped her chin on the palm of a hand. "This project is beginning to fill me with a disturbing melancholy. I can't work if I'm not happy."

Lisa watched von Stroheim's face. It was chiseled in stone. Then, quite suddenly, it was wreathed in a smile that was as genuine as a four-dollar bill. "All right, Greta. You shall have your Alysia Hoffman." He turned his back on her and crossed to a window. Garbo looked at Lisa and winked. "Alysia Hoffman. Wasn't she pretty big in Germany years ago?"

"Yes, she was pretty big."

"She's now willing to be a stand-in?"

"She's poverty-stricken. She has put her pride in mothballs. Maybe you could also give her a part. It would be a blessing."

"Yes. I'll see what I can do. I'm sorry I made such an unnecessary fuss."

"That's all right, I enjoyed the exercise. Shall we continue?"

Garbo's return to films made headlines across the nation. Hedda Hopper and Louella Parsons were almost hospitalized with the gastronomic disturbances brought on by having to eat their words. Louis B. Mayer, in a rage at the news, decided to cancel several contracts, and so Joan Crawford, the formidable Norma Shearer and Myrna Loy were soon to join the exodus from the lot. Newspaper editors were almost buried under a mountain of letters decrying the profligacy of a five-million-dollar budget for a film in these dire times. Garbo was criticized in several quarters for accepting the one-million-dollar fee, though she had every intention of donating a large percentage to several war agencies—except the Red Cross because she didn't like the color. The Internal Revenue Service was drooling at the prospect of the taxes it would collect from all participants in *Joan the Magnificent.*

In Herb Villon's office, he and Arnold Lake carefully studied the personnel lists clandestinely slipped to them by Lisa Schmidt with every name submitted to Washington for security clearances, regardless of their standing in the industry. Arnold lit a cigarette and asked Villon, "Why do you suppose Garbo was so adamant about getting Alysia Hoffman as her stand-in?"

"You heard what Lisa said. A clash of wills. Score one for the great Garbo."

"They aren't great buddies. Garbo knew her briefly in Sweden back in '25. Until the de Acosta broad brought them together again, they hadn't been in touch."

"Garbo isn't big on being in touch."

Arnold blew a smoke ring. "Nineteen twenty-five. Garbo's in Germany making a movie, *The Joyless Street*. Nineteen twenty-five. Hitler's Nazi party is emerging on the political scene."

"Now come on, Arnold, you're not trying to tell me you suspect some kind of a link then? She was young, naive, an innocent kid of twenty. She knew from nothing. She's even apolitical today. She doesn't vote."

"She can't. She's not a citizen."

"Oh."

"Oh. I'm not accusing the lady of anything. I'm just thinking out loud. Anything's a possibility in the espionage racket. So she's finally getting to meet Guiss tonight."

"Yeah. Dinner at his Bel Air mansion. Very secluded, highly guarded."

"Just the two of them?"

Villon referred to a memo on his desk, information from Lisa Schmidt by way of Martin Gruber. "There's to be Guiss's girlfriend, Risa Barron. Then there's the guy who's supposed to be co-producing, Werner Lieb. Figureheads, of course. Von Stroheim has already made it quite clear that he's in charge."

"They sat still for that? No ego problems?"

"Not according to Lisa, and that girl of yours is good, she's very good," said Villon.

"Strange. Still, these are only the preliminaries. Let's see how they behave when the actual shooting is underway. Who else?"

"Gustav Henkel, who wrote the first script." Villon rubbed his chin.

"There's a second script?"

"It's in the works now. Bertolt Brecht's writing it."

"What's a Bertolt Brecht?" asked Arnold.

"Brilliant German writer. *The Threepenny Opera* and a couple of others."

"What's *The Threepenny Opera?*"

"I don't know. I never saw it. And then there's William Haines."

"The movie comic? He hasn't been heard from in years. Where'd he crop up from?"

"After he was washed up in pictures eight years ago . . . too many boys. . . ."

"One of *them?*" Arnold might have been alluding to an alien from outer space.

"Right. He took to interior decorating, and thanks to Joan Crawford, who gave him his first crack at it, he's found a whole new career for himself. He's one of the few guys Garbo ever spends any time with."

Arnold asked, "What about the secretary, Martin Gruber? Do you think he'll be in attendance?"

"Very much so."

"That's good. I don't trust him."

"That's good and you don't trust him. So what's good about it?"

"It's good because he passes on the word to Lisa."

"For a nice price."

"And it's bad," elucidated Arnold, "because informers are rats to begin with and I don't trust any of them. Somewhere along the line he'll foul up."

"Maybe he won't."

"All informers foul up sooner or later. They get too cocksure and they then slip up. Guiss has run through an impressive list of secretaries, not one of whom came to a good end except one broad named Ilse Koch who's running a concentration camp in Germany." He rubbed out the cigarette in an ashtray. "It'll happen to Gruber. Sooner or later he'll make a dumb move. They always do." He shook his head sadly. "They always do. Aren't any of the picture's big hitters invited?"

"You mean von Stroheim or any of the cast? Not as of this memo from Lisa. I think Guiss wants Garbo all to himself. He's a big fan of hers. He drools at the very mention of her name. Come to think of it, what wouldn't I give to be there myself?"

Six

It was later that afternoon when von Stroheim had his meeting with Alysia Hoffman. Lisa Schmidt had efficiently tracked down the actress after getting her phone number from Mercedes de Acosta, and the shrewd de Acosta had advised Alysia to stay home near her phone, foreseeing an imminent summons to meet the Emperor von Stroheim.

Still pretty, thought Lisa as the receptionist ushered Alysia into the office. The crow's feet are beginning to appear around the lips, the eyes have a strange hardness, probably brought on by the hell she must have gone through getting out of Europe, but her height and her coloring are right.

Von Stroheim was surprisingly gentle with her and the actress was admirably composed. "You are an old friend of Greta's?" He was slapping the riding crop gently against the palm of a hand. Alysia told him they first met in Sweden nineteen years ago when she had traveled from Germany, where work was scarce, to see if there were opportunities in the burgeoning Swedish film industry.

"You speak Swedish?"

"In silents it didn't matter," she said with a smile. "Once my career shifted into high gear, I made films all over Europe. France, Italy, Austria. We all did."

"Of course," said von Stroheim. "I myself had many offers, but I was too busy here then. So you want to be Greta's stand-in."

"I need the job."

"Your height and your coloring are right. You agree, Schmidt?"

Lisa considered saluting him but swiftly thought better of it. "I think Miss Hoffman would be perfect."

"Women." He spat the word contemptuously. "You always stick together."

"I wouldn't take that as gospel," said Lisa slyly. She could see the actress was now uneasy.

"Don't be impertinent." His eyes shifted back to Alysia. "Miss Garbo suggests it might be generous on my part to also find a supporting role for you in the film."

"She's so kind."

Von Stroheim refrained from making an ugly comment about the star, still bristling over her firm demand that Alysia be hired as her stand-in. "There's a small but interesting part that you might be right for. A heretic, a follower of Joan. She gets stoned to death by a mob." He said it with such relish, Lisa expected him to cackle with glee.

"I know I can handle it."

"Of course you can." He was on his feet and pacing. "But remember this, I'm a fanatic where realism is concerned. I plan to use *real* stones." He bent over, his face against hers. *"Real* stones. You don't flinch? You don't protest? You don't say thank you very much but I'll remain behind the cameras? I don't frighten you?"

"Mr. von Stroheim," she said calmly, evenly, in a voice that won Lisa's admiration, "after what I've been through these past two years, nothing can frighten me."

He was back behind his desk. "I am satisfied. You are hired. Miss Schmidt will make the necessary arrangements. You will have the shooting schedule a week before we will begin."

"And when is that?" She couldn't disguise her anxiety. Lisa wondered if she ought to offer to lend her a fiver.

"That will be decided within the next few days. We only moved into the studio at the beginning of the week. We are still casting. And I'm awaiting the decision as to whether or not we shoot in Technicolor." He said with gusto, "Can you imagine what Technicolor will do to enhance the battlefields? Rivers of real red blood flowing past the dead and dying, the agonizing cries of the horses as they are brought down and crippled, the geysers erupting from decapitated bodies, oh by Christ this will win me the Academy Award those bastard cretins have denied me for years!"

Lisa Schmidt excused herself and hurried to the bathroom to throw up.

"Lottie." Garbo spoke her housekeeper's name gravely. Garbo was in her Spartan bedroom sipping a cup of bouillon, preparing to bathe and dress for Guiss's dinner party. Her housekeeper was laying out the ensemble Garbo had chosen to wear. "The coming months may be very difficult for you."

Lottie looked up from the slipper she was polishing. She said quickly, "Nothing is easy, I always say."

"Ah Lottie, so you are a philosopher!"

"Miss Garbo, from the time I decided to go into service, I knew there'd be a rough go ahead of me. Do you mind if I tell you how I feel about myself and others in my position?"

"But no, of course not. It would be such a privilege!" She might have just heard she'd won the Irish Sweepstakes.

"Well, ma'am. I think we're unique. It takes a special kind of person with a special kind of personality to decide to wait on others. You know what I mean? Maids, butlers, housekeepers, we're special. And good ones are damned hard to find, as you well knew when I finally landed on your doorstep."

"Oh how well I knew. You have been so good to me, Lottie."

"And you've been good to me, ma'am, and very generous. I'm the only domestic in Santa Monica who owns a frayed chinchilla opera wrap." She smiled, which she did infrequently. "I love parading around in it in my bedroom."

"Oh I'm so glad you like it. I wore it in *The Temptress,* oh, so many years ago. . . . It was a silent movie."

"I know. I saw it. You were great." She cleared her throat. "You see, we go through hell when we're interviewed for jobs. When I came here two years ago . . ."

"Is it that long we're together?"

"Yes ma'am, two years. I remember telling my parole officer, 'Garbo'll never hire me. When she hears I did time in San Q. she'll get turned off.' "

"But I didn't, did I? I was so fascinated! To have someone working for me who had the courage to poison her husband." Garbo's hands were clasped and the look on her face was sheer ecstasy.

"Poison. The son of a bitch took forever to die."

"Oh you have found that out too? How difficult it is to rid ourselves of people who no longer amuse us. Oh, if only I had your courage. How you must have agonized before finally lacing his soup and cocoa. . . ."

"Hot chocolate."

"How you must have agonized before deciding to kill him."

"I didn't agonize at all. The only thing that drove me nuts was how long it took him to die. Of course I'd read up on poisons and then it was hell getting enough of it to prove fatal. He would just slurp and slurp and ask for seconds and I tell you, that was so damned frustrating! I really began to get this feeling of inadequacy. I mean some friends were with me when he suddenly looked up from my special lentil and split pea number . . . the bacon and the thinly sliced leeks are what do the trick," she winked conspiratorially, "and he gasped, 'Holy shit!' and fell face down into the soup. Well I was so relieved I said, 'Well it's about time' and my big mouth did me in. Anyway, I had a real shrewd lawyer—Isadore Marino, half wop, half Jew—and he saved my neck. Anyway, you were saying? The road ahead's going to be a tough one to travel?"

"Yes. A very tough one. Joan is a very difficult character to interpret, and von Stroheim is a very difficult man to work with. And I must cope with this strange smorgasbord of co-producers and writers and musicians and refugee actors, all of them undoubtedly with a method all their own. *Ach* God how we shall clash!"

"My money's on you, Miss Garbo." Lottie was attacking the slipper with fresh gusto.

"Is it really?"

"Miss G., when you're on the screen, everybody else gets wiped off."

Garbo was sad. "Not always. Constance Bennett stole my last film from me. And she's such a terrible person."

"It was such a terrible picture. Oops. Sorry."

Garbo laughed. "Don't be sorry. Your honesty is refreshing." She looked at her wristwatch. "I must start dressing. The car will be here soon."

"You've got plenty of time. It's picking up Mr. Haines first. He's miles from here."

"And now they tell me the film will be in Technicolor. I have never filmed in Technicolor. I will insist on tests. Technicolor is for musicals. I must make sure I do not look like Betty Grable." She crossed to her floor-length mirror and stood with her back to it. Then she looked over her shoulder at her mirror image, a familiar Grable pinup pose. After a few moments she was satisfied she would never look like Betty Grable.

Guido's was an unprepossessing and inexpensive Italian restaurant near the Goldwyn Studios. In a quiet booth toward the rear of the establishment, Lisa Schmidt sat having dinner with Alysia Hoffman, both having settled on veal piccata and spaghetti.

"This is so good," yummy-yummed Alysia. "How really kind of you to invite me to dinner."

Lisa twirled pasta on her fork. "To be perfectly honest, I didn't have anything else to do and I was in no mood to sit around my apartment reading Fannie Hurst. Anyway, I like the way you handled von Bastard."

"Is he really all that terrible?"

"I'm sure it's mostly affectation. He's still living back in the old days when he made his masterpieces, even though the studios butchered them."

"Still, how many directors have been capable of those masterpieces. *Greed* is soul-stirring."

"Are you Jewish?"

"What?" Alysia almost dropped her fork. Lisa's steady gaze never left her companion's face. "Jewish? Me, not at all."

"Then why did you have to leave Germany? You're still a big star there. Why give up your career to go through an exile's hell?"

Alysia sipped some Chianti. "How do I make you understand?"

"It's not important, really. I mean I'm a nosy bitch and I know I ask too many questions. . . ."

"No no no no. It's a perfectly valid . . . valid, is that right? Valid?"

"Perfectly valid." The veal was stringy.

"Good. It's a perfectly valid question. You see, Lisa, Jews are not the only refugees fleeing Hitler. I was . . . how do you put it? Yes a rebel, a firebrand. I rebelled against the Nazis and what they stand for. And I was very outspoken. Foolishly, I suppose."

"I think you have guts you haven't used yet, Alysia."

"Guts?"

"A colloquialism for strength, bravery."

"Ah yes. How nice. Thank you. So I was outspoken and I started to get into trouble. Goebbels, who has control of the movie industry, warned me time and again about my overactive mouth. Well, I thought I was big enough a star to pooh-pooh his threats. But *ach* no. Soon I was being followed, my mail was being opened, and they investigated lovers who might have been yids and some of course were. . . ."

Lisa placed her fork quietly on her plate and studied the woman who was talking and eating ravenously.

"And then they were questioning my friends."

"What about your family?" asked Lisa.

"I have no family. I was married back in '26 but that didn't last very long. I haven't the vaguest idea where he is now. His name was Heinrich, he was a prize fighter."

"Like Max Schmeling?"

"Oh not so good, though Schmeling has capitulated to the Nazis, I heard, when I was in Mexico."

"It must have been hell getting to Mexico."

"Of course first I tried to get a visa into the States, but I was rejected. I made a deal to do a movie in Spain for Franco, a terrible script but it was a good excuse to get me out of Germany. While in Spain, I had an offer to do a film at the Cherubusco Studios in Mexico City with Luis Buñuel. You've heard of him?"

"Yes. He's brilliant."

"Well, this film never got made. But it wasn't cancelled until after I arrived in Mexico City, so I was safe. The authorities let me stay. But there were no more offers of work. My money was running out and soon I was scratching about to survive. It wasn't easy."

"But it helped improve your Spanish."

Alysia laughed. "I was already fluent in Spanish. I was always very good with languages. Soon my English will be better, no?"

"I'm sure it will be. Dessert?"

"Oh I don't think I have room!"

"You've got to try Guido's zabaglione. It's one of the few things on the menu he doesn't have to be ashamed of. Go ahead and order, I have to call an actor I've been trying to get in for an interview tomorrow. Order me a pot of espresso, honey."

Alysia lit a cigarette as she watched Lisa cross to the wall telephone on the opposite side of the room. So beautiful, she was thinking, so very beautiful. Somehow she seems miscast in the role of von Stroheim's assistant. Still, it was good to be friendly with her. She had learned soon after her arrival, you can never have enough friends in Hollywood.

William Haines, former MGM star and now a successful interior decorator, couldn't contain his enthusiasm for the young man chauffeuring this splendid limousine. And it was splendid indeed. There was an impressively stocked bar and a small refrigerator with hors d'oeuvres, peanuts and pretzels, several decks of cards, a checkers set and a chess set and a Parcheesi game. And there was the young man propelling the car smoothly on the road to Garbo's home in Santa Monica. That profile, those broad shoulders, a splendid youth, even if his accent was by way of the Katzenjammer Kids.

Haines crossed a leg and began his campaign. "What's your name?"

"Ludwig."

"Like in Beethoven?"

"Oh yes, sure."

"How long you been in this country?"

"Not long."

This is hard work, thought Haines. But quite a challenge to an old campaigner. "How long have you been driving for Mr. Guiss?"

"Long time."

"Oh. So you worked for him in Europe."

"Long time I leave Europe."

Haines thought, Get your story straight kid, I'm not. He was beginning to enjoy himself. "Since you're not long in this country and you've been driving a long time for Guiss, what have you been doing in between?"

"Driving."

Smart cookie, thought Haines. "Is that all you do? Drive?"

"I only drive."

"Don't you ever putt?"

"Pardon."

"Forget it. Inside joke." He slumped down in the seat. He was looking forward to seeing Garbo but not looking forward to the cast of characters he suspected would be their dinner companions. Like anyone else with a healthy inquisitive nature, he was glad for the opportunity of a firsthand look at Albert Guiss. He was glad Garbo was going to do Joan, because there was something he wanted her to try and do for him.

He hated asking another favor. After his fall from grace eight years earlier when Mayer set out to destroy his career and his credibility in Hollywood (I wonder if the old bastard ever found out I serviced Gable a few times?), Garbo had been one of the few people who had come forward on his behalf. At the time he had thought she was barely aware of his existence. They'd been working on the same lot for almost ten years, but never once did she say a word to him when they passed each other. True, she was aloof to just about everybody else in the studio ("She's very shy, Bill. Don't be upset.") but after all, didn't she appreciate he was Metro's court jester? Always clowning around, always saying campy, outrageous things about everyone and anyone, until he himself was the butt of cruel laughter and derision.

Joan Crawford had always been a pal and remained steadfast. Of all people, Norma Shearer, wife of the powerful Irving Thalberg, went out of her way to ask him to their parties despite her husband's admonitions. But the morning Garbo called and invited him to lunch, *that* was overwhelming. Thinking about it now it brought tears of sentiment to his eyes. She'd invited Marion Davies, Salka Viertel and Mercedes de Acosta and they all got high on gin and orange juice. And thanks to Davies, there were kind words in Louella Parsons's column a few days later that he was now busy considering offers from independent producers. Independent indeed. Poverty Row. And he did a few quickies because he needed the money. Greta had come through, another of her occasional contradictions. She wasn't an iceberg. She did have a heart. He once saw her pat a gatekeeper's little boy on the head. That must have taken quite a bit of courage on her part.

"What? What did you say?" The chauffeur had penetrated his reverie.

"We're here. Miss Garbo's."

"Oh. Well that was fast. I'll go get her." As he opened the limousine door he said over his shoulder, "Now don't you be funny and drive away or I'll cry."

The chauffeur watched Haines cross to Garbo's front door and press the doorbell. Under his breath he voiced a vicious epithet and then sat back, dreaming of returning to Germany and the war, dreaming of the glory that would be his when he would decimate the enemy with bullets and bayonets and hand grenades and his bad breath.

"Oh Billy, darling, Billy, why are we going to this suffocating dinner party?" She was sipping vodka on the rocks and Lottie was ready for him with his usual scotch highball.

"Because you have to and I'll be your immoral support." He raised his glass high. "Here's to absent friends."

"That is so sad," said Garbo. "It makes me think of obituaries. The first thing, Billy, the first thing I read in the newspaper is the obituaries." Her face was wreathed in a pained expression. "Do you read the obituaries too?"

"I'd be dead without them."

"Have you noticed lately how many obscure nobodies are dying? It shouldn't be permitted. Shall we be fashionably late to the dinner?"

"Yes. Come sit by me." She joined him on the couch. "Sweetie, you've been a wonderful friend."

"Oh please."

"You have. And I'm remembering you in my will."

She laughed. "Please don't. I have so much of my own. Leave it all to your boyfriends!"

"Those ungrateful sons of bitches? Let them all starve to death. Now let's get serious."

"And Roebucks?" He glared at her. "Don't you like my little joke?"

He patted her hand. "It's adorable. Let's be selfish and keep it to ourselves."

"I should never tell jokes. Salka always says I don't know how to tell a joke. You're getting impatient with me. Don't. I'm very nervous about this dinner. I'm very nervous about the whole project. I've made a terrible mistake and I can't back out. If only I was capable of a nervous breakdown."

"Greta, please listen. I'm doing so well with the decorating that now I'd like a chance to branch out."

"Branch out? But where?"

"Set dressing. Let Cedric Gibbons and the rest design the sets, but let me choose the furniture and the decorations. Don't you think I'd be great at it?"

"Oh Billy. You could be great at anything you choose to be. You could be president of the United States if you weren't so odd."

He took her hand. "Speak to them about me. Maybe they'll give me a chance."

"You mean von Stroheim? God." She was up and pacing. "I've already defeated him on the hiring of Alysia Hoffman." She told him about the Hoffman problem that had been decided in her favor. "Now you ask me to defy the dragon in his cave again." The look on his face was now so little-boy-lost, she put her drink down and threw her arms around him. "I enjoy defying the dragon. It stimulates my adrenalin. I will do it for you, Billy." She withdrew her arms, looked at her wristwatch, and stood up with her arms outstretched. "How do I look?"

"Sensational."

"You think the cut of the back is not too daring?" There was no back and it was indeed daring.

"There are them in which it could bring on a heart attack."

"I will fascinate Albert Guiss?"

"From what I can gather, he's already fascinated. Interested in landing yourself a mysterious billionaire?"

"I don't know." Lottie held the front door open for them. "I have to see what he's like in person. I must study him very carefully. I must converse with him. And he already has a mistress."

"I'm sure there's room for one more."

"Ha ha ha ha. Don't wait up for me, Lottie. I'm not sure when we'll be back. If God is good, it will be early. So darling, just set out a glass of milk and some Hydrox for me."

Seven

The atmosphere was charged with electricity. Garbo felt it the minute the massive front doors swung inward to admit her and Haines. She had felt it when the limousine drove up the road leading to the castle, and it was surely a castle, in the exclusive Bel Air compound. When they reached the wrought-iron gates that protected Guiss's castle from unwanted invasions, an electric eye found them and triggered the gates to open. Haines was surprised there were no armed guards. On the other hand, the ramparts and turrets of the magnificently imposing structure could easily camouflage any number of dangerous gunmen.

Garbo commented with equanimity, "Very impressive." She had had her share of castles. She had portrayed Sweden's Queen Christina. The limousine parked at the bottom of a wide flight of stone stairs.

Haines counted thirteen as they ascended. Sweet. Somebody isn't superstitious. And then the massive doors swung inward. There was no burst of organ music and Haines was disappointed. But there was a butler and six footmen and four maids and Haines wondered if they had been choreographed.

Surely the butler was from Central Casting, a replica of the celebrated character actor Gustav von Seyffertitz. His accent was pure Herman Bing, Bing being an actor who played mostly comedy waiters. The manner in which he directed the footmen and maids had to be a God-given gift. His name was Kriegman and when Garbo was curious about his origins he told her his family originated in East Prussia.

Kriegman led them up a long flight of richly carpeted stairs, surrounded on both sides by tapestries whose values she was sure had to be estimated in six figures or more. She whispered to Haines, "A bit ostentatious, don't you think?"

Haines nodded and wisecracked out of the side of his mouth, "The big showoff. What do you bet the main dish is frankfurters and sauerkraut."

"Oh I do hope so!" she said with sincere enthusiasm, "I do hope so."

Haines asked her, "Where'd he get the extras holding the spears?"

The spear holders loomed ahead of them standing on each side of a set of double doors to which Kriegman was leading them. They wore black uniforms trimmed in gold braid, and Haines wondered when a soprano and a tenor would appear. As the three approached the doors, the guardsmen became animated and swung the doors open. Garbo suppressed a gasp. The huge room was a dazzling display of somebody's magnificent taste.

"I'm jealous," said Haines.

Garbo knew at once that the tall, elegant, impeccably dressed man approaching her with arms outstretched was Albert Guiss. "We meet at last," he said in a voice meant to be seductive. "I'm Albert Guiss." He kissed both her hands. "I see you are overwhelmed by the decor, but you dwarf it all with your own special brilliance."

What a line, thought Haines, I'll bet it has caught a lot of fish. He could see Garbo was somewhat hypnotized.

"Mr. Guiss . . ."

"Oh please. You must call me Albert."

"And you must call me Greta." Her teeth sparkled like her smile. "I want you to meet my friend, William Haines."

"You must call me Billy," said Haines with his celebrated smirk which some innocents accepted as a smile.

Guiss stepped between them and took Greta by her right arm and Haines by his left, and guided them to the other guests. "Here Greta, seated on the love seat, are your two producers, my watchdogs, heh heh. Risa Barron and Werner Lieb."

Lieb stood up and bowed stiffly from the waist. Risa Barron extended her hand, which Garbo touched slightly in friendship. Haines wondered how Risa could raise her arm, it was so weighted down with jewelry.

"Miss Garbo, at last," said Risa Barron.

"Greta. Everyone must call me Greta. After all, we'll be working together for many many months, we must be on first name terms and become good friends."

"You wonderful woman," said Risa, sounding like steam escaping from an overheated radiator. Billy Haines wondered how so many ugly features could be set together to create a fascinating face. She had a long nose, wide mouth, a pointed jaw, and eyes with an oriental cast to them. Her lips were ruby-red luscious and there was just enough eye shadow to give her a suitably mysterious aura. This babe knew how to sell herself, thought Haines with admiration, and he could understand her conquest of Guiss. The head happened to be on top of a very stunning body.

Werner Lieb was something else. Haines thought he should be an assistant checker in a sausage factory. He was pale, slim, wore his evening clothes with panache and managed the monocle in his left eye like a veteran of monocle managing. He too kissed Garbo's hands, gushing, "This is a dream come true, Greta. To meet you at last, but also to work with you."

"Thank you. I'm sure the film will be more than memorable for all of us. But look, Billy! An old friend of mine!" Gustav Henkel stood near the massive fireplace holding a glass of champagne. She prayed he wouldn't smile. He did. "This is Gustav Henkel, who wrote the script which Brecht is rewriting and it does not seem to bother Gustav. See! He's always smiling!"

"Kriegman!" barked Guiss, "Drinks for Miss Garbo and Mr. Haines." She asked for champagne and Haines asked for his scotch highball.

Greta took Guiss by the arm and walked him around the room, pausing here in front of a Tintoretto, here in front of a Picasso, here in front of a Renoir, then a Degas, and surprisingly, a few moderns like Max Ernst and Salvadore Dali. "What a fabulous collection, where did you acquire your unique taste?"

Haines wished he could find out where he acquired his unique fortune, but instead busied himself in small talk with Risa Barron. "I'm stunned by your emeralds."

"Thank you. What about the rubies?"

"Blood red and knockouts." He wondered if they were gifts or trophies.

"Billy? Weren't you the movie star William Haines?"

"Ah yes, back in the Middle Ages."

"But why did you stop acting? You were sometimes funny."

"That about sums up my career, sometimes funny." He accepted his highball from Kriegman, who he thought could use a pair of roller skates to get across the enormous length of the room to Garbo before her champagne went flat. Haines asked, "Excited about producing the film?"

"Who wouldn't be? It was so wonderful of Albert to ask Werner and myself to co-produce." She bent her head and whispered, "Of course there is von Stroheim to contend with." She laughed. "I have contended with worse. Hitler and Mussolini, for instance."

Haines was impressed. "You knew them?"

"But of course," was the matter-of-fact reply. "Hitler wanted me for his mistress. This was before Eva Braun. But I could not live with a man who sucks his teeth. Now there is a price on my head. I am on Adolf's hit list. Oh well, let us hope that is not my epitaph."

Garbo was saying to Guiss, "Yes, I am delighted we'll be shooting in Technicolor, but von Stroheim must make tests of me. I must have Westmore devise suitable makeup for the color cameras. After all, Joan can't be rosy-cheeked with orange lips and green eyes. True, the script is witty here and there, but Joan must never be an object of fun, or else how can we expect the audience to sympathize with her?"

"That is absolutely true. I'll convey all this to Von. By the by, now that we're doing it in color, he's thinking seriously of your suggestion to show her burning at the stake."

She laughed. "Of course he would. Joan roasting in glorious Technicolor. A riot of cerise and orange and brown and yellow. Von Stroheim will revel in it. Someone who knows Technicolor must be brought in to advise and moderate him. He will go too far."

"I know that." Guiss lit a cigarette and then jammed it into a pearl-studded holder.

They were standing next to a Botticelli. "Albert," said Garbo, "how come you settled on von Stroheim? Don't get me wrong, we worked together once as actors and it was fine. But no one else in the industry will buy him as a director, and along comes generous you giving him five million dollars to play with."

"He better not play with them." The eyes were narrow and the voice rasped and Garbo took this as a sign the man was not playing the dilettante. The sudden flash of cruelty sent a small tingle jogging down her spine. In a more genial tone he advised her, "Believe me, von Stroheim was not my first choice. First I approached the most obvious man for the job. Cecil B. deMille."

"Of course, he's so deliciously banal."

"He did consider it for awhile. It seems he'd already done Joan as a silent with Geraldine Farrar."

"Oh yes? I must try and find a print. I'd like to see it."

"I've seen it. Terribly primitive. I tried many others, even Alfred Hitchcock, but he waved me away with a very cryptic, 'There's no suspense.' "

"True. Like *Hamlet,* there's no changing the ending," Garbo said.

"My next choice was Josef von Sternberg."

"And he wanted Marlene to play Joan."

"Oh not at all. They barely speak these days. He wanted Ingrid Bergman."

"Oh? But you couldn't get her?"

"I didn't even try. I wanted you and only you." His voice was smooth and seductive. He took her hand and caressed it while his eyes devoured her face. "And now I have you."

"You have Greta the actress."

"And if I want Greta the woman?"

She saw another guest arrive and cut him off abruptly. "Who is that man?"

"Martin? Martin Gruber is my personal secretary. He is late because I sent him on an errand. Martin! Come meet Greta Garbo." Gruber hurried across the vast expanse to join them.

"Poor man," said Garbo. "He'll be out of breath before he reaches us. What a vast expanse. Was it once a ballroom?"

"No, the ballroom is in the north wing. I plan to throw a party there when the film completes shooting."

"That could be years from now," she said mournfully.

"Miss Garbo! Miss Garbo! You leave me speechless." Gruber never shut up. "I am one of your greatest admirers. I have seen all of your films at least a dozen times."

"Really? No wonder you wear such thick glasses."

"I have an awful myopia." He said to Guiss, "I have taken care of the matter."

"Good. I see Kriegman has opened the doors to the dining room. We are ready to serve dinner."

"*Wunderbar.* Frankfurters and sauerkraut!"

"Frankfurters and sauerkraut? What ever gave you such an idea? Such food is for walk-ons and extras," he said proudly. "Tonight I am serving pheasant under glass and chateaubriand and trout Marie Antoinette."

Garbo said, "I have never heard of trout Marie Antoinette."

Guiss smiled suavely and said, "That's trout with the head removed."

They found their place cards and were seated. Garbo could tell, from the number of empty glasses and the amount of silverware at each place setting, that it was going to be a very long evening. Already before her was a plate of paté de foie gras with truffles and gherkins ("alive alive oh," whispered Haines to Risa, who was quite befuddled) and she dug in with her celebrated enthusiasm.

"Greta does love her food," said Haines to Risa. "If she'd been born in Africa, she'd have been a cannibal."

Martin Gruber feasted in equal parts on the paté and Garbo's face. He was enchanted by her throaty laugh, the way she seemed so riveted to every word Guiss said and how she gently touched his sleeve every so often. If she was insincere, he was witnessing a truly magnificent performance.

Werner Lieb cursed Guiss silently for having placed him next to Gustav Henkel. The scenarist preferred his fingers to a fork and showed little respect for the royal truffles. He ate with his mouth open, accompanied by ugly sucking noises that recalled to Werner the ugly noise of the automatic dredges on his grandfather's farm in Alsace. Werner attempted conversation. "Have you seen any of Brecht's rewrite?"

"I tried to. He was very polite when I introduced myself. Then he threw me down the stairs."

"I heard he's terribly temperamental."

"And he's always chomping on those stinking cheap cigars. And his teeth!" Henkel displayed his own and Werner shuddered. "He has the most awful teeth!"

The soup and the fish elapsed uneventfully. The pheasant under glass caused Haines to comment, "I saw them move." Risa Barron covered her mouth with a hand and excused herself for a few moments. Haines looked across at Garbo and Guiss. He could tell they were holding hands under the table. He wondered why that disturbed him.

He heard Martin Gruber asking, "Do you ever contemplate returning to acting, Mr. Haines?"

The question always annoyed him and so he chose a facetious reply. "Why no, I'm thinking of becoming a spy."

His voice carried and he was the cynosure of the table.

Garbo dabbed at her lips with her napkin. "A spy, Billy? You? But that is impossible. You can't keep a secret! Ha ha ha ha ha!"

The only other person who joined her laughter was Billy Haines.

Eight

Within less than a week following the dinner party, Greta and Guiss were the talk of the town. Louella Parsons gushed on her Sunday night NBC radio program at nine-fifteen, following Walter Winchell's breathless and breathtaking fifteen minutes, "Greta Garbo and Albert Guiss seem to have found each other. They met last week at a dinner party to celebrate the start of filming Garbo's comeback film, *Joan the Magnificent*. Since then, my spies tell me they're inseparable. The mysterious financier was seen with Greta at the House of Westmore where she and von Stroheim, who is directing the film, were devising a color makeup for Greta. I've been told some evenings Greta and Guiss take long walks on the beach at Santa Monica where Greta has a pleasant little house. Of course they could only be discussing the film which begins shooting tomorrow, but if they're deeply involved in a romance, well, your Guiss is as good as mine."

Although it was a Sunday night, the Samuel Goldwyn studio was a beehive of activity. Technicians were under pressure to get the lights and the sound equipment installed to von Stroheim's satisfaction. The shooting schedule had to be rearranged to accommodate Peter Lorre's Dauphin, as Jack Warner needed him for a film with Sydney Greenstreet. Because of the use of Technicolor, a heavier-than-usual electrical board had to be installed. The Dauphin's palace had been beautifully designed by Cedric Gibbons, who had been borrowed from MGM with the surprisingly benevolent blessing of Louis B. Mayer. When Garbo heard this, she frowned and said to William Haines, "He's up to something. Why is he being so accommodating? First he lets me have Adrian to design my costume and then he permits Gibbons to design the sets."

"I heard he almost had apoplexy when he heard I was decorating the interiors."

"Which reminds me, Billy. No chintz. They didn't have chintz in those days."

"They didn't have much else either," said Haines glumly, "but they were big on sackcloth and ashes."

Garbo paraded around her dressing room. "I like my costume. Don't you?"

"How'd you get him to get rid of the padded shoulders?"

"My shoulders never need padding. I have a good frame." She studied herself with admiration in the full length mirror she'd demanded be installed and was satisfied.

Haines asked, "What's going on between you and Guiss? Lolly told her millions of listeners tonight that she suspects you're a hot and heavy item."

"We're a little heavy but we have not yet gotten hot." She sat before her dressing table mirror and lit a cigarette. "Don't you think he's very attractive?"

"If you like the type. I think Nils Asther would be better casting."

Garbo exploded. "Oh never never. Nils is too passive. He doesn't have a commanding personality. He does have the softness Albert occasionally displays, especially when we walk on the beach and he talks of the future." She was examining her fingernails. "He plans someday to retire to South America. To Brazil. He has bought a jungle and a river. He is having the jungle cleared and building a little city there."

"You mean a little kingdom, don't you?"

"Sometimes I don't know what I mean and sometimes I don't know what he means. He is such a mass of contradictions."

"Do you think he's in love with you?"

An arch look spread across her face. "But of course he must be. I am so fascinating. I am Garbo, the siren from Sweden. Have you forgotten all the men I've conquered and destroyed in my films? Wasn't I a superb Mata Hari?"

"I couldn't keep a straight face during your love scenes with Ramon Novarro."

"Neither could we. He thought of one of the dress extras he wanted and I thought of a trip to Europe and somehow we got through it. It looked awfully good on film, though, didn't it?"

"Because you made it look good. Christ, when you kiss a man, you devour him."

"But Billy, if you are truly and deeply in love with a man, when you kiss him, it must be to devour him. When I love, I love with an all-consuming passion." She attacked a thumbnail with an emery board. "I've forgotten what it's like, it's been so long. What time is it?"

"It's a little before ten."

"I'm tired. I want to go home."

"What are you hanging around for?"

"Peter Lorre. The first scene tomorrow is the dauphin and Joan. I wish Erich would reschedule it for after lunch. It's such a difficult scene. We need to rehearse it." There was a knock at the door. "Maybe that's Peter now. Come in!"

Lisa Schmidt entered. She said to Haines, "I thought I'd find you here. Himself is on the set and yelling. That miniature statue of the nude gladiator you've placed in the Dauphin's bedroom displeases the master. He wants you on the set."

"That son of a bitch has no eye for beauty!" exploded Haines, "All he digs is distortion and ugliness and physical disabilities. Watch, you just watch. Most of the extras will be blind, missing an arm, missing a leg, dwarfs and midgets and God knows what else. I try to liven things up a bit with a gorgeous, muscular gladiator and he blows a gasket. Which I'm sure is all he blows." As he stormed out to beard the lion on the set, he shouted, "The next scream you hear will be mine!"

They watched his exit, and Lisa asked in a tired voice, "Do you mind if I sit for a minute?"

"Please! Would you like some coffee? It's hot in the thermos there. There's also a thermos of chicken soup and hot chocolate. My housekeeper is a treasure."

"Maybe some hot chocolate."

"Hers is wonderful. She poisoned her husband with hot chocolate."

Lisa said, "I'll have some coffee. Some for you?"

"No, I'll brave the hot chocolate. I think Lottie's poisoning days are long past. Anyway, we are good friends."

"How does it feel to be going back to work?"

Garbo said, "Well, I am no longer a slumbering volcano."

Lisa's face was a study as she poured the hot drinks. "Don't you think this is a strange setup?"

"Strange? Oh, it's a bit exotic. Risa Barron fascinates me. She and Werner Lieb know absolutely nothing about film making and display their ignorance with such authority. And those jewels she wears! My God! They must be worth a king's ransom. But I like her. She amuses me. She doesn't seem to object to the way Albert pays court."

"Between you and me," Lisa said, carrying the cups of hot liquid to the dressing table, "I think she's a taxidermist's masterpiece. Who are these people? Where did they spring from?"

Garbo's eyes were wise and inquisitive as she took the hot chocolate from Lisa. "Are you curious or is von Stroheim curious?"

Lisa laughed and sat. "We're both curious. Guiss is Guiss. I think what little is known about him is all we'll ever know. Or have you managed to penetrate his armor?"

"Oh I don't know. He had to have a mother and father, didn't he?" She contemplated the hot chocolate, which was thick and creamy. No wonder the late Mr. Lynton so greedily went to his death. "Who they were, I haven't the vaguest idea. You know what I think? I think from early in his life he had ambitions to be a very rich and very powerful man. I think he's totally ruthless. . . ."

Lisa feigned shock. "My dear!"

Garbo smiled. "I haven't told you anything I haven't told him. He admits he is self-made, that he always wanted wealth and power, and to attain such vaunted ambitions one has to be at the very least quite ruthless. I'm ruthless. Von Stroheim is ruthless. Every major star and executive in this business, every politician and dictator in the world is ruthless. You have to be to achieve your ambition. But once achieved, you have to be even more ruthless to hold on to it. Take Risa Barron. She told Billy Haines she was once friendly with Hitler and Mussolini. That Hitler wanted her to be his mistress. Do you think this is possible?"

"Why not? With a woman like that, anything could be possible. Jesus, those jewels."

"I'm sure Jesus had nothing to do with it."

"Hitler and Mussolini. That's quite a parlay. And yet she's here on the lam from the fascists."

"I'm sure that was Albert's doing."

"Now that Europe's overrun by the hounds of war, I wonder how badly Guiss has been hit in the pocket. I read somewhere he had vast holdings in Germany, Italy, France and Austria that have been confiscated."

Garbo laughed. "I'm sure he has plenty left."

"I'm told you like Bertolt Brecht's revised script."

"Oh I think it's very good. Now it has wonderful shadings. The lightness doesn't overpower the darkness the way it did in Henkel's. Now it is much more of a parable and therefore it is much more powerful. I'm very excited by it. Oh God, by the sound of that knocking I can tell it's Werner Lieb at the door. I suspect he has trained with the military." Lisa followed Garbo with her eyes as the actress crossed to the door. "He walks, he talks, he bows from the waist and he knocks on doors like a true *Junker.*" She opened the door. There stood Werner Lieb. "I was right. Come in Werner, what's the problem?"

"I came to see your costume." Garbo struck a pose. "Very good, very good indeed." Lisa wondered if he slept with his monocle. She wondered a lot of things about him and his friends and was anxious to share her theories about these people with Arnold Lake and Herbert Villon.

"Dear God, what is all that shrieking?" Garbo went back to the door, opened it and saw von Stroheim brandishing his riding crop in pursuit of Billy Haines. "Oh look at those two fools! And look at Peter!" Peter Lorre, a cigarette dangling out of the side of his mouth, his script under one arm, his jacket hanging somewhat precariously from his shoulders, his hands shoved deep into his pockets, approached Greta's dressing room.

He said wearily, "Von Stroheim will suffer a stroke at the rate he's going." He surveyed her dressing room, which was actually a portable caravan. "I don't suppose I shall be afforded such a luxurious accommodation."

"I didn't ask for it," Garbo said defensively, "Guiss insisted I have it."

"Is he any good in bed?"

"Why don't you ask someone who's been to bed with him? Come in. You're late."

"I was beating up my wife. I do it every Sunday night when she listens to Lolly's program. She loves it. It makes her sleep better. She's an occasional insomniac." He walked past Garbo, who closed the door and returned to the dressing table. "Hello, Werner. Have you done any co-producing yet?"

"I can assure you Risa and I will be quite competent."

Garbo hoped the venom in Lieb's voice wouldn't prove fatal. Lisa Schmidt was trying to make a quiet exit. Garbo asked, "Are you leaving us, Lisa?"

"I thought I might rescue Billy from von Stroheim."

The smoke in his eyes from his cigarette didn't impair Lorre's vision. When Lisa spoke, he turned to look at her, acknowledging her presence for the first time. He liked what he saw. A beautiful figure, gorgeous legs; he couldn't quite see her face as she went to the door. He wondered quickly if she was amenable and available.

"Lisa?" he asked, "Who is Lisa? Why haven't I been introduced to Lisa?"

"I warn you, Lisa. Mr. Lorre is a predatory monster. Possibly because he was brilliant as a child molester in *M.*"

Lorre said through a cackle, "But Lisa hardly looks like a child. Turn around, dear, and let's introduce ourselves."

Lisa's fists were clenched. Her mouth was dry. She said a silent prayer, a prayer that begged God to strike Peter Lorre with some form of amnesia, and then she found a lavish smile and turned around and faced him. "Nice to meet you, Mr. Lorre."

"Oh, I am overwhelmed! Such beauty! Such ravishing beauty! Greta, aren't you jealous?"

"No. She makes little of her looks, which makes her a very wise young woman."

Lorre walked to Lisa, slowly, studying her face despite the smoke continuing to cloud his eyes. She folded her arms and waited.

Werner Lieb was intrigued by Lorre's performance. He sensed the actor was up to something, playing a game of cat and mouse with Lisa, who indeed looked as though she was about to be eaten.

"I think we have met before," Lorre finally said. "Haven't we?"

Lisa said firmly, "I have never met you before, Mr. Lorre. I'm quite sure of that."

"I know I'm not crazy. It was about a month ago. Maybe longer."

"I have to go, Mr. Lorre. You'll have to excuse me."

"Now don't be in such a rush. Wait a minute. Let me think." He took the cigarette out of his mouth and held it between two fingers. "Yes, of course. It was *you.*"

Garbo said with impatience, "Oh Peter, stop playing with Lisa. Make friends with her. You'll need her. She handles von Stroheim superbly and is very useful. Lisa, don't look so frightened. Peter is harmless. Peter, behave yourself."

Lorre was annoyed. "I *am* behaving myself. Lisa and I have met before. We have, haven't we, Lisa?" She said nothing. She wished lightning would strike, she wished anything would happen that would rescue her, the way she had prayed to be rescued that night she was pursued on the beach. "We have and we know you know. Remember that night on the beach, Greta?"

"Oh? So now I'm a part of this plot?" She flung the emery board aside. "Peter, will you please sit down and let Lisa get on with her work. Go, Lisa. I'll see you later."

Lorre suddenly raged. "I will not be treated like a fool, Greta! This is the girl on the beach, the one who was running away from something and hid behind your rose bush under your patio. The one your neighbor saw, what's his name . . . ?"

"Saloman." Greta looked perplexed.

"That's right, Saloman. And she sought refuge with me. She asked to use the phone. When Toth . . . you know . . . with the private police guard we pay for . . . when he knocked at my door I hid her in the closet in the living room . . . the one my wife never looks into . . . and when I went to speak to Toth, she fled. Damn it!" He pointed an accusing finger at Lisa Schmidt as Werner Lieb watched the scene with fascination. "You are that woman! You're the one who was being chased and it had something to do with the house in which that strange Wolheim family used to live."

Desperately, Lisa found a laugh. "I'm awfully sorry, Mr. Lorre. You have me confused with someone else. I have to go." She fled.

"But I swear on my wife's head," Lorre insisted to Garbo and Lieb, "she's that woman! Look how frightened she is!"

"I'd be frightened too if you attacked me the way you just attacked Lisa. Oh really Peter, I remember that night now. I'd had drinks with Marion and then went home. I did see someone running from under my patio but only vaguely because of the blackout. And as for you, you were probably in a cocaine haze at the time. There probably wasn't any girl at all."

"Are you trying to convince me I'm insane? I tell you," he said, pointing a finger in the general direction of Lisa Schmidt's departure, "that was the woman who came to my house that night!"

"This is all terribly dramatic," Werner Lieb interrupted, "but I must get back to the office. I promised Albert I would see your costume and report to him. I shall tell him I'm very satisfied with it."

"It doesn't matter. I'm satisfied. That is all that is important where this costume is concerned."

Lieb clicked his heels and gave her the stiff bow from the waist. *"Auf wiedersehn."* To Lorre he said, "Nice to see you again."

A strange look crossed Garbo's face. She saw Lorre react to Lieb's acknowledgment in much the same way Lisa Schmidt had reacted to Lorre when he fingered her. She watched Lieb depart, wondering if he also slept with his body stiffly rigid. Lorre flung his script down on the couch and crushed his cigarette in an ashtray. When they were alone, Garbo asked, "When did you meet Werner Lieb?"

"Lieb? You mean the man who just left? I've never met him before."

"He said, 'Nice to see you again.' "

Lorre shrugged. "Recognizes me from my film. Everybody recognizes me. I never have any privacy anymore."

"Peter," said Garbo gravely, "you've never met him before the way Lisa Schmidt claims she's never met you before." She picked up a hairbrush, faced the mirror and began stroking. "You all intrigue me so. How exciting life is becoming again. I suspect now this film is a hotbed of subterfuge and hidden secrets. Possibly dangerous secrets. Am I right, Peter?"

He was lighting another cigarette. "Let's go over our lines, Greta. I'm a little shaky with them."

"Peter," she spoke his name softly, "I suspect you're a little shaky with things other than your lines." Then in rich tones, she spoke her dialogue, having in just a few days committed Brecht's rewrite to memory, " 'My dauphin, my prince, majesty, I am a simple peasant girl who has come to serve you. My voices . . . my voices have entrusted you in my care . . . oh sire . . . you must believe in me. . . .' "

She didn't hear Lorre speaking his opening lines. She was wondering what she could believe in. She was worried, and she was a little frightened. She needed to talk to Salka Viertel.

Nine

Lisa Schmidt needed to talk to Arnold Lake and Herbert Villon. She found Arnold at his hotel, the Garden of Allah on Sunset Boulevard and Crescent Heights. It had once been the estate of the tempestuous and exotic silent-screen star Alla Nazimova. When she fell on hard times, the estate was sold and remodeled into a series of lovely bungalows and was often home to such literary luminaries as Robert Benchley, Dorothy Parker and Robert Sherwood and a smattering of stars when they were between spouses. It had a popular bar and anyone who didn't drink was looked upon with suspicion or denounced as subversive.

Arnold in turn left messages at various checkpoints for Herb Villon, who was soon located and joined Arnold and Lisa at the Garden of Allah.

In Arnold's bungalow, they listened to Lisa's story of her encounter with Peter Lorre. When she was finished, she said, "I don't think anyone saw me leave the lot. I should go back." Neither of the men said anything. "Werner Lieb is one of Guiss's henchmen. I'm positive he was in that meeting at the beach."

Arnold finally spoke. "Going back could be dangerous."

Villon said, "Not going back could be equally as dangerous."

"That's what I think," said Lisa. "I'm all for going back and brazening it out. What's the worst that could happen to me?"

"You could be killed," said Arnold. Lisa exhaled and reached for the scotch on the rocks he had poured her. "We know for sure there's something subversive and dangerous going on there. The movie's a front for some kind of undercover activity and it smells to high heaven."

Lisa didn't try to disguise her skepticism. "You don't think Garbo would be part of any subversive activity, do you?"

"Who knows? Look at some of the fifth columnists we've been rounding up. Respected politicians, pillars of society, the country's one big nest of underground communist activity."

"I thought the reds were our allies," offered Villon.

"Lately, but with that mother Stalin, who the hell can be sure of what's next? Garbo lived and worked in Germany back in 1925. That picture she made . . ."

The Joyless Street," said Lisa.

"Didn't she tell you some of those actors she worked with became Nazis?"

"She did," Lisa said, then added hotly, "but there were some of them who didn't. All that happened years after Greta came to the U.S. I tell you she's absolutely apolitical. She's not dumb, but she's not all that smart. What she is is shrewd and very self-protective. The lady isn't quick to give an inch, let alone a yard. I think she's been suckered into this deal and it was easy to land her because she was so confused and upset at parting company with Metro."

Arnold persisted, "What about her romance with Guiss?"

"I don't think she's serious. It amuses her. She finds him and his gang funny. You heard me, to her they're one big collective laugh. She's getting a million bucks, she can afford to laugh." Lisa lit a cigarette. "What I'm wondering is, how does Lorre fit into this scenario? I heard his name mentioned out at the beach. It was he who brought Guiss's offer to Garbo."

"And it was her two girlfriends who steamrollered her into finally giving the deal the nod," added Arnold.

Villon asked Arnold, "Viertel and de Acosta are clear, aren't they?"

"On the surface it would seem so," said Arnold. "They contribute heavily to antifascist causes. They work on a lot of committees. Garbo doesn't."

Lisa said, "Garbo is Garbo. I told you. She's not a political animal. You know she's always shied away from the public eye. She's very choosy about who she associates with. I'm amazed that she seemed to take to me immediately."

"You're a direct line to von Stroheim. She can make use of that."

"She tried to get Lorre off my back. She didn't have to do that."

Villon asked, "This Werner Lieb . . ."

Lisa said, "I'm sure he believes Lorre. That bunch took after me that night, at least some of them. Now they see I've weaseled my way into the production. I'm sure they see me as a threat."

Arnold said gravely. "Look, toots, you're my girl. You're important to me. But we're painted into a corner. If you disappear, they'll be positive we're on to them and we'll never learn another thing."

"Don't you think I know that?" She smiled. "Garbo could be a help."

Villon chuckled. "Are you crazy? Garbo doing cloak and dagger, you've got to be kidding."

"She sure knows how to dig for information, and get it." Lisa sipped her drink. "Keep her in mind. She's going to cross-examine me about Lorre's accusation. What do we do about him?"

Villon said, "I know him slightly. We sweat it out in the same steambath on Thursday night where the celebrities go. You know, Bogart, Eddie Robinson, Vic McLaglen. . . ."

Arnold said sharply, "You be careful of McLaglen."

"That big idiot?" Villon had an incredulous look on his face.

"Don't you know he has his own private army? Cavalry. They meet every week and go through maneuvers and they wear black shirts. McLaglen's Irish. And the Irish are very much on Hitler's side. Hitler's ships and submarines use Irish ports for repairing and refueling."

"I'm flabbergasted," said Villon.

"It's no big secret. Northern Ireland especially. They've no love for Great Britain. They want their independence."

Lisa said, "They're lousy lays."

Arnold smiled. "We can send you to Mexico until this blows over."

"The food doesn't agree with me. No, gentlemen, the lady is frightened shitless but she's going back to the studio. If anything happens to me, at least you know where to investigate, and who to investigate. By the by, this Risa Barron, the one with all the jewelry, she blabs to everyone she's been intimate with Hitler and Mussolini."

"So was Guiss." Arnold had them riveted. "And Hitler offered Garbo his world if she'd return to Germany."

Villon said, "Well it's obvious she turned him down."

Arnold Lake was very tired. "It's way past my bedtime." He asked Lisa, "You sure you want to go back tonight? Why don't you go home and get some sleep. You start shooting tomorrow and it's going to be a rough day."

"You're right. I'm going home. And I'll be in constant touch." Arnold kissed her. "And Arnold, be sure to tell my mom and dad how much I love them."

"When?"

"I don't know. Just in case."

"I got here as fast as I can. Driving in the blackout is hell. Is there any coffee?" Salka Viertel took off her suede jacket and flung it across the back of a chair.

"In one of those thermoses." Garbo watched her friend opening and closing thermos bottles until she found the coffee.

"What's wrong? You're terribly tired. You should go home. What time's your first scene?"

"It will be in the afternoon now. Von is having serious technical problems. Sit down, Salka. I have something very important to discuss with you." She told her of Lorre's confrontation with Lisa Schmidt.

"So? What do you think this means?"

"I think it means something dangerous is going on around here. Maybe Lisa Schmidt is involved in some kind of espionage."

Salka laughed. "You overdramatize everything."

"Oh no. Not this. Not her being pursued on the beach, if it really was her. How we suspected that Wolheim family were a strange bunch because none of them resembled each other. Guiss and his cohorts. And this ugly Gustav Henkel. I don't think he ever wrote the first script of *Joan.*"

"Now really, Greta."

"I mean that, Salka. What writer doesn't fight to do his own rewrite? He calmly sits back and lets them put Brecht on the job? He only wrote one draft. At least demand the right to do the first revision. But no, he sits back without uttering a peep and lets himself be replaced. And Risa Barron with that fantastic jewelry that would make Maria Montez suicidal with envy. She brags about having relations with Hitler and Mussolini. And Guiss. How he woos me. How he promises me the world if I would become his lover."

"Have you?"

"I don't want the world. It's difficult enough to cope with Hollywood." She thought for a moment. "They sent Peter with the offer. They hired von Stroheim when they supposedly couldn't get anyone else, not even von Sternberg. But he's Jewish."

Salka was confused. "What are you getting at?"

"But von Stroheim's also Jewish. He and Joe weren't born to their 'vons.' They added the 'von' to their names when they were getting started, to make themselves sound like aristocracy. Ha ha ha! How does Greta von Garbo sound to you? Ha ha ha!" Garbo settled into a chair and crossed her legs.

"It sounds perfectly awful. Greta, what are you suspicious of?"

"These people. I think they are frauds." She leaned forward and hypnotized Viertel with a steady, piercing look. "Why did you and Mercedes work so hard to convince me to play Joan? Why?"

Salka tasted her coffee, but it was tepid. She put the cup back in the saucer. "We did it for von Stroheim. The three of us—Peter, Mercedes and myself. Without you, there would be no film. Guiss set up this project to get to know you. He is besotted with you. He has been for years."

"Five million dollars for Greta Garbo? Compared to that, what Louis paid me was a pittance and yet I'm a millionaire. Fate is so ridiculous. Really, Salka. Is that all? Is that really all? Has Guiss severed all his ties with the Germans?"

"I don't know anything about that. I don't know what his ties were to the fascists other than he claims they've confiscated billions of dollars worth of his property. You should know more about this then I do! Louella says . . ."

"Oh to hell with Louella." She was on her feet pacing, wringing her hands agitatedly, eyes darting about like a frightened sparrow's. "I have such a presentiment, Salka. Something terrible is going to happen."

"You're being very silly, Greta. What's in those other jugs? They must still be hot. Drink something and then we'll go home."

"Home. Yes, home. Home to my Lottie. She'll protect me."

"This hot chocolate smells wonderful."

"That's how Lottie poisoned her husband. With hot chocolate."

"Forget the hot chocolate. Ah! Chicken soup. It smells scrumptious. What's Lottie's stand on chicken soup?"

"Oh Salka, Salka. I fear for Lisa Schmidt. Oh that fool Peter. Accusing her in front of Werner Lieb."

"Lieb?"

"Another flunky. Supposedly the co-producer. If anything happens to Lisa . . . oh God!" She flung herself onto the couch. "I should go to Switzerland, where they're neutral." She looked up at Salka. "Believe me, Salka, there's something rotten going on in this studio. I'm not sure what it is, but it's going on. I have a lot of thinking to do. Yes, I think I'll go home."

Ten

Lisa Schmidt an American agent?"
Albert Guiss swallowed the information Werner Lieb gave him,
took time digesting it, and then said, "Are you quite positive?"

"Quite positive, no. We have only Peter Lorre's word for it."

"Lorre's word, as we well know, could be as shaky as his health.
Well, if she was the spy at the beach house, she couldn't have heard
all that much. We only discussed the film. Risa, what do you think?"

Risa was thinking she'd rather be in her bed getting some much-
needed beauty sleep. She was staring at Gustav Henkel, who seemed
to be dozing in his easy chair, but with that one you never could tell.
Perhaps he was feigning sleep. He did that frequently when conver-
sations were too deep and over his head. "I think Gustav is asleep."

Guiss looked at the writer and smirked. "Perhaps not, perhaps his
mind is wandering."

"Not without a road map," offered Risa, who didn't like Henkel.
She thought him common and quite ordinary and wished he'd do
something to improve his teeth.

"Let's get back to Lisa Schmidt. What's your opinion of her, Risa?"

"Opinion? Opinion? Opinion about what?" When she was tired, she became testy. "Is she a spy? How do I know? I only know her from her work on the film. And she's terribly competent. I know von Stroheim is very pleased with her and when his wife visited the studio last week I don't think she was happy to see that Lisa is so beautiful. Greta seems to like her."

"Very much so," added Lieb as he polished his monocle with a silk handkerchief.

"That's important," said Guiss. "Greta relates to so few people."

Henkel spoke softly. "She asks a lot of questions."

Guiss arched an eyebrow. "Greta?"

"Lisa Schmidt."

"What kind of questions?" pursued Guiss.

"How long have you been here. Where do you come from. Where is your family. How long have you been with Guiss, et cetera, et cetera, et cetera. Sometimes it is dizzying to be evasive. I have made up a whole new biography of myself just to satisfy her inquisitive nature. And the trouble with that is, I can't remember half the lies I fed her."

"If she's really an agent with the FBI, your lies have been recorded and examined. And you're such a brilliant liar I'm sure they find your information most entertaining."

Werner Lieb interrupted. "What's the decision about Lisa Schmidt?"

"To act against her now on such flimsy evidence as Lorre's would in my opinion be very stupid." Guiss had left his position behind his desk and crossed to a map of the world framed and hanging on the opposite wall. The inevitable cigarette in the pearl holder was clenched tightly between his teeth. He studied the map and then, with his hands clasped behind his back, paced the length of the study. "We must do nothing that could jeopardize the progress of the film. We are heavily invested in it and our fate lies in the hands of an egomaniacal director and a manic-depressive actress who, for reasons beyond my capabilities to understand, wants to become a saint."

Risa was studying Guiss. Lover, friend, philanthropist, sadist, bon vivant. Truly a mess of contradictions. She said, "Albert, I agree with you. To move against Lisa would mean doing away with her, and that will mean the police, and if she is really an agent, it will mean the FBI. We don't desire the company of either. We will just have to be very careful. We must somehow convey to Lorre we'd appreciate he keep his mouth shut about her. . . ."

"That's easy," said Werner. "We could threaten him with an inferior brand of narcotics. Like that swamp grass some crooked dealers import from Central America."

"It's after one A.M.," Risa announced impatiently, "let's get some rest. We have to be on the set early tomorrow morning. It's the first day of shooting. How about that? We have at least accomplished that! I feel very satisfied!"

"Feel very satisfied," said Guiss, "but don't feel smug. Good night."

At seven the next morning, Martin Gruber met Lisa Schmidt for breakfast in the coffee shop in Culver City, a safe distance from the Goldwyn Studios, where no one would see them. She told him about the encounter with Lorre, and although Gruber was crumbling his prune Danish instead of eating it, this was the only sign that the incident disturbed him. His mouth wasn't twitching the way it usually did when something disturbed him. She continued with her meeting at the Garden of Allah and, when that dissertation was over, finally took a bite of her buttered bagel.

Gruber motioned to the waitress for coffee refills, asked her to remove the destroyed prune Danish and replace it with a whole-wheat muffin with raisins, cream cheese on the side. They sat in silence for a while, Lisa chewing her bagel, Gruber looking past her outside the window at the Metro studio down the street, which was beginning to hum with activity. Finally he spoke. "Guiss had a meeting late last night. Werner, Risa, Henkel. I was excluded."

"Does that worry you?"

"Not at all. It's a pattern I've grown to recognize. When it's top secret, I'm excluded. But I can guess you were the topic under discussion." He waited until the waitress deposited his muffin and refilled their coffee cups, and then continued. "Guiss is too clever to engage the police or the FBI right now. Sooner or later it will probably have to happen, but not right now. Because if they suspect you're an agent and kill you, then they are the targets of an investigation they positively don't want. After all," he said with a coy smile, "remove the *r* and the *e* from *corpse* and you are left with *cops*."

"Cute. Give me a bite of your muffin, it looks good."

"Help yourself." He sipped his coffee. "Go to the studio. Do your job. From the snatches of conversation I hear, you are liked. Certainly Risa Barron speaks well of you."

"Well that's a comfort."

"You see, it would be easier to ease you out of your job, and avoid the possibility of your continuing to be a threat to them, than kick over a hornet's nest by killing you. To me that would be the sensible move to make."

"If they haven't thought of it themselves, don't you suggest it."

"Don't be ridiculous."

"Supposing Lorre doesn't let up on me?"

"It is my calculated guess, Lisa, he will no longer be a problem. Lorre is himself in a difficult situation. His family and his wife's family are still in Europe. Lorre's a Jew. As long as he plays nice with Guiss, the families are protected."

"He's been trying to get them out, you know. He's petitioned the White House."

Gruber chuckled. "The White House! It's too late for that even with the White House. The war is on and there's no exit for anyone except Axis agents." He looked at the wall clock over the counter. "Isn't it time you got going to the studio? I know Guiss will soon begin to miss me. I'll get the check. We go dutch as usual, yes?"

"Next job you get, ask for an expense account."

* * *

At the studio, Goldwyn and Sophie Gang were crossing the lot to the set of *Joan the Magnificent*. He always greeted the start of a new rental production by personally appearing on the set to welcome the newcomers. He liked activity; he thrived on seeing actors and technicians going about their business with alacrity. Making films was his life's blood and he was as enthusiastic about rival producers' projects as he was about his own. "Sophie, take a memo."

"I don't have my book."

"So put it in your head!" he fumed. "Later we'll take it out. I have come to a mountainous decision. I am going to make *The Brothers Karamazov*."

"But Mr. Goldwyn . . ."

"Don't 'but' me. My decision is final and irreverent!"

"But Mr. Goldwyn," said Sophie in a voice that pleaded with her boss to be reasonable, "the exhibitors are begging for women's pictures. They're up to their projectors in war films. They want romantic films desperately. Pictures the women will go to see!"

Goldwyn thought for a moment and then his face brightened. "All right! So we'll call it *The Sisters Karamozov*! And what's more, I'll offer the part of Grushenka to Greta! How's that?"

"Mr. Goldwyn, how can there be a Grushenka if you change them to sisters? She's the woman they fight over."

He thought for a moment. "Then Greta can be one of the sisters. I'll change Grushenka to Goldfarb and offer it to John Wayne. There's that rotten von Stroheim. A terrible man, a very terrible man. Hello Erich! Why haven't you come to visit me and say 'hello'?"

Von Stroheim had been about to chew out an electrician. "Well, Sam. Nice of you to drop by."

"Tell me Erich, do you know *The Brothers Karamazov?*"

"Not intimately." He collared the electrician, who was trying to sneak away.

"Come by and see me. I may have for you an interesting preposition. Where's Greta? I don't see Greta. Look at all the people, Sophie. This is really going to be a gigantic *eppis*. Look at all the actors and actresses! It looks like a *Who's What* of everybody who isn't working. Look Sophie, there's Eddie Quillan, and Mary Gordon. Over there, look. Cliff Edwards, by golly. What's Ukelele Ike doing in a movie about Joan of Arc?"

"Maybe they found out she liked ukeleles," said Sophie.

"You think so?" He stared about in amazement. "And this set. It must have cost a pretty penis. You know, Sophie, I think I should get to know this Albert Guiss. What do you think?"

"That's him over there with his entourage." Guiss was standing in the middle of the set accompanied by Risa, Werner and Gustav Henkel. Sophie led Goldwyn to the group.

Goldwyn confronted Guiss. "Mr. Guiss, I assume. Let me introduce myself. I am Samuel Goldwyn. I own this studio."

Guiss and Goldwyn shook hands, and then Guiss introduced the others.

Goldwyn continued, "Good luck. A lot of good luck. I smell you're going to have a big hit on your hand."

"Thank you very much, Sam."

"Of course you won't see much until the war is over and you can display it in Europe. In Europe Garbo is a big name, a very big name. But until then, you'll have to march time." Goldwyn was warming up. "I want this to be a big hit for you so it'll be like spitting in the face of that rotten Hitler. Joan will conquer the way the Allies will conquer. They'll push Hitler's nose into horse menus and then I have already suggested they put him in a cage and take him on a world tour for everyone to see. They should charge of course a nominated sum and they'll clean up a fortune. Maybe I can get in on it." He hadn't noticed he had lost his audience.

Sophie remarked as they strayed away, "A very strange bunch."

"Not very polite either," huffed Goldwyn. "Come, let's give a hello to Greta."

Garbo was pleasantly astonished as she entered her caravan dressing room followed by Lottie Lynton and Mercedes de Acosta. "Look at all the flowers! It is like a greenhouse in here! Look Mercedes, there is no room for us! And champagne!" There were at least half a dozen buckets of champagne and bottles of whisky, vodka, and brandy. "And look! Chilled caviar just the way I love it with chopped onions and chopped eggs and sour cream. Lottie, my dear, please fix me one."

Mercedes said, "Look over here, Greta. From Louis B. Mayer, a plate of chopped liver. He probably made it himself."

Garbo struggled out of an oversized sweater. "We must send the flowers to hospitals. But the food we keep for ourselves," she said as she rubbed her hands together and grinned lasciviously. She took the caviar-drenched biscuit from Lottie and bit into it greedily, while Mercedes found her a paper napkin to wipe the dribble from her chin.

"Greta Garbo!" said Goldwyn sternly as he and Sophie entered. "Why aren't you making Joan of Arc for me instead of for these foreigners?"

Garbo liked the man; she had always enjoyed him and his beautiful wife, Frances. She swallowed her mouthful and said, "You didn't ask me. And besides, you already did Joan years ago as a silent. Why would you want to do it again?"

His hands were spread out palms up, "So I can hear her talk! I don't mind chewing my fat twice. Didn't I make *The Dark Angel* and *Stella Dallas* twice? Who sent all these flowers?"

Out of the side of her mouth Sophie warned him, "You sent the white carnations."

Like the crack of a whip, his tongue worked. "Look at my white carnations, aren't they municipal?"

Garbo giggled. "Very municipal, Sam. They're also lovely. But I am so perplexed by all these flowers! Is this for starting a new movie or for a funeral?"

Lisa Schmidt had entered unobtrusively. Mercedes was the first to spot her and admire her beauty. She didn't know her but she assumed she was on the production staff. She very much liked Lisa's beauty. Mercedes wanted to know her better. She heard Garbo babbling about flowers and food and what a trial the first day of shooting can be and would Lottie pour her some hot chocolate and, as she held up the hanger holding her costume, asking Goldwyn and Sophie if they didn't approve, which Sam didn't but held his tongue, and then she commanded Mercedes' attention and Mercedes cooed that it was an absolutely brilliantly designed piece of work and it might just start a new fashion in women's clothes.

That sobered Garbo. "I never thought about that. It's possible, isn't it? Remember how popular I made the pillbox hat and I never saw a nickel of it. Mercedes, remind me to have a talk with Adrian."

Now Goldwyn took the spotlight with his offer for her to do *The Sisters Karamazov* and he would forever puzzle why this brought on a fit of hysterical laughter. Sophie Gang came to his rescue reminding him they were late for a writers' conference with Aldous Huxley and Christopher Isherwood. Goldwyn explained to Garbo, assuming she might never have heard of the two British writers, "They're not only good writers, they're allies. I want them for a picture I'm planning about Bulldog Drummond, you know, the safecracker." (He actually pronounced it "Bullfinch Drumming.") "It's for my new comedy star, Danny Kaye."

"Mr. Goldwyn, we're late," insisted Sophie.

"So what? I'm Sam Goldwyn, aren't I? Did I know one day I'd be Sam Goldwyn? I have a right to be late. Goodbye, Greta. Good luck. I'll bet Mayer sent the chopped liver. And if I'm right, hire a food taster. Stop pulling my sleeve, Sophie!"

When they were out the door, Garbo slumped into a chair. "Yes, the first day is always the hardest. And the last day is always the saddest. But we are a long way from the last day. So Lisa Schmidt, why do you stand there like a lonely mouse?"

Lisa came forward. "I wouldn't dare compete with Sam Goldwyn for your attention."

"Where did you disappear to last night? I tried to find you."

"I was tired and very upset by Lorre. I went home."

"Yes, Peter was very naughty teasing you the way he did. Peter is not celebrated for his handling of women." She crossed to the dressing table and sat there. She saw Mercedes ogling at Lisa. "Oh where are my manners?" She introduced the women to each other while Lottie unpacked several cases of knickknacks which Garbo brought to make the dressing room homier and cozier. There were canned goods and an assortment of cheeses, cold cuts and biscuits to be stored in the kitchenette closets and refrigerator. Garbo was asking Lisa, "Was that you on the beach that night?"

Lisa smiled. "It certainly was not."

Mercedes wondered, "What do you suppose this woman was spying on?"

"Not 'what,' but 'who.'" Garbo thought for a minute. "Whom?" She dismissed it with a wave of her hand that just missed swatting a fly. Mercedes repeated her question.

Garbo said, "That house has been uninhabited for a long time. I wonder who owns it?"

Lisa wanted to blurt out, "Guiss!" but said, "Wouldn't the real-estate people in the neighborhood know?"

"Possibly," said Garbo. She told Lisa, "A very strange family lived in the place for a while—the Wolheims. It's really such an ugly mess, the sort of architecture they favored thirty years ago. Strange house, strange family." She was cleaning her face with cold cream. "Salka and I saw them a few times. A father, a mother, three sons and a daughter. But they bore no resemblance to each other."

"Maybe the children were adopted," suggested Mercedes.

"Salka thought that a possibility too. Funny," she said, wiping the facial cream away with tiny pads of cotton, "they materialized from out of nowhere and then disappeared just as mysteriously. You know, come to think of it, it was early last December when I realized the house was no longer occupied. I remember asking my neighbor, Mr. Saloman, if he knew when the strange family had left and he said they went away December eighth. The day after Pearl Harbor was attacked."

Lisa, who had helped herself to some of Lottie's coffee, said in a strange voice, "Maybe they were German spies." Lottie flashed her a look, startled.

"Do you think it possible?" asked Garbo, eyebrows arched.

"In this town, anything's possible. Do you recall what these people looked like?" Mercedes was applying a match to a cigarette.

"Not really. The youngsters were very ordinary looking. The mother, the mother come to think of it . . . ," she laughed with a faraway look in her eyes, ". . . come to think of it she looked as though she would be perfect as a *bürgermeister*'s wife. You know, the wife of a small-town mayor in Germany. I saw lots of them when Mauritz and I used to motor about on weekends when I wasn't needed in front of the camera. And as for the father, I only once got a real look at him." She repositioned herself so she no longer had to address their reflections in the mirror.

Mercedes asked. "Tall, short? Thin, fat? Bald maybe?"

"You know something funny. Now I know who Kriegman reminds me of."

Mercedes asked, "Who's Kriegman?"

"He's Albert's butler. That night at dinner, when I first saw Kriegman, I had a sense of déjà vu. Yes, he reminded me of Wolheim. Isn't that funny?"

Eleven

Kriegman."

Arnold Lake was in Herb Villon's office. "Who's Kriegman?" asked Villon.

"Guiss's butler. That was Lisa I was talking to."

"So I gather. No repercussions from last night?"

"Not from Lorre. He hasn't shown up on the set yet. He doesn't film until the afternoon. Lisa saw Gruber this morning. He felt the same way about Lisa's position as I do. They won't make a move against her until they think it's absolutely necessary. He's sure they don't want the cops or us feds swarming all over the place."

"What about Kriegman?" Villon persisted.

Arnold told him what Lisa had heard from Garbo about the possibly bogus family Wolheim. "I think we ought to have a look at that house."

"Easy enough to get a search warrant."

"Why don't we just go down there and pry open a window?"

"Shame on you, Arnold. That's breaking and entering. That's against the law. It's a felony."

Hands on hips Arnold asked, "You've never done it before?"

"Sure I have. But this house is on Santa Monica Beach. Right there with the big moving-picture stars. Very classy. The Santa Monica boys aren't crazy about us common L.A. cops. We have to move carefully and legitimately. I'll arrange the warrant. There's a pretty good seafood joint out there. We can lunch."

On the Goldwyn lot, in the office prepared for Albert Guiss, Guiss was seated at his desk dictating a memorandum to Martin Gruber. "And in addition," he said very precisely, clipping each word like a stock coupon, "I think it will be detrimental to the film to overpublicize it so early in production. What's the word for that, Martin?"

"Hype."

"Hype." He was amused. "Hype. I like it. Where was I? Oh yes." He leaned back in his chair and contemplated the ceiling. It was a warm day and the windows had been opened wide. He could hear the activity outside and, as someone never before associated with a motion picture, felt that wonderful charge so exclusive to the initial excitement of producing a film. Soon he would be bored to tears with the endless waiting for scenes to be shot, the daily chore of sitting through the rushes, especially von Stroheim's rushes, which would be thousands of feet of film more than other directors would need to shoot. He continued with his dictation. "True, the return of Garbo and von Stroheim is big news, but we can assume in time the excitement will die down and be replaced by other items of fresh interest, so that we can do a concentrated campaign after the picture is completed and edited to everyone's satisfaction and ready to be released, of course, with great hoopla. . . . Hoopla is right?" Martin nodded. "With great hoopla and fanfare and hopefully to huge profits."

"Shall I read this back to you?" asked Gruber.

"Not necessary. You're always very competent."

"Thank you." Guiss wasn't always given to compliments. Praise didn't come easily from his lips.

"Lisa Schmidt."

"Nice girl," said Gruber, without taking his eyes from his notebook.

"I'm not asking for a recommendation, Gruber. I want you to find out who she is."

Gruber was an excellent actor and had once trained with the immortal Max Reinhardt. But Reinhardt found his backside too fat and his voice too thin. "I can get her employment application from personnel."

"I want you to dig deeper then that, Gruber."

"I see. May I ask, is there something suspicious about her?"

"If there weren't, would I be asking you to find out more about her than a ridiculous job application can tell us? Most of those are lies anyway."

And most of what I find out for you, herr Guiss, will be lies anyway, but oh what the hell, they will be delightful lies.

Guiss continued, now at the window and looking out, all the while jamming a cigarette into the favored pearl holder. "Get to know her. Take her to lunch. Perhaps she's uninvolved. Play up to her. That shouldn't be difficult with someone as beautiful as she is. Look. There she is now." Gruber joined him at the window. Lisa was facing Peter Lorre.

Lorre said to her with wide-eyed innocence, the look he employed in films after committing a particularly gruesome murder, "You must forgive me, Miss Schmidt. How could I have embarrassed you the way I did last night? I am so ashamed of myself. I was so upset when I got home I kicked my wife in the shins."

"No matter, Mr. Lorre. It was a bit startling, the idea of me on a beach in a blackout in the dead of night. I'm like the old maid who looks under the bed before she gets into it at night."

"Oh really?"

She was beginning to understand why there were women who found him attractive. He was rumored to be having an affair with a German refugee actress, Kaaren Verne, and she was an exquisite beauty.

"Perhaps one night soon you'll let me come and help you look under the bed?"

She laughed a very husky laugh with difficulty.

"Perhaps one night you'll look under your bed and there I'll be waiting to be trapped. Anyway, Greta was very upset with me and she was right. There was a hunter's moon that night and there was a lot of mist and perhaps I had indulged just a soupçon too much of happy powder. Now we are friends, yes?"

"Of course."

"Good. Why don't we go to the Mocambo tonight? Xavier Cugat's orchestra is playing and I do a dangerous rhumba."

"I'm sorry. But we're working late tonight."

"Oh yes. Of course. I forgot. Oh dear. Greta will be furious. We're supposed to be rehearsing. I'll see you later." He scurried off like Alice's White Rabbit, very late for a very important date.

Something made Lisa look up to the second floor of the executive building. She saw Guiss and Gruber at the window, looking down at her. Guiss didn't notice Gruber's wink. Lisa hurried away.

In Garbo's dressing room, Lottie Lynton asked, "Shall I prepare lunch, Miss Garbo?"

"Let's wait until Mr. Lorre gets here, if he'll ever get here," she added with irritation. "Mercedes, you're so sweet to keep me company but if you have better things to do . . ."

Mercedes was too intrigued with intrigue. "Are you thinking Kriegman was really Wolheim?"

"Oh? Are we back to that again? Good. I like puzzles." She put a finger to her cheek. "Was Wolheim also Kriegman? I don't know. I didn't say he was, did I? I think I said Kriegman reminded me somewhat of Wolheim. Lots of people remind me of lots of people. There were times when I thought Goldwyn and Mayer were interchangeable, but then I'd remind myself how much they despise each other, so they can't be the same person."

"I wonder who rented to the Wolheims? That party ought to know something about them. They had to have references."

"That's an interesting thought." She clapped her hands. "Oh Mercedes? Do you think we should play detective?"

"It's an idea," said the small woman, puffing on a cigarette.

"It could also be dangerous," commented Lottie from the kitchenette.

Garbo reminded Mercedes, "Lottie knows a great deal about detectives. She doesn't like them."

There was a knock at the door and Peter Lorre didn't wait for an invitation to enter. "Something smells good," said Lorre.

"Yes it does," said Garbo with a frown. "Lottie! I thought I said to wait on lunch until Mr. Lorre gets here."

"He's here, isn't he?"

Garbo shrugged. "Never argue with a treasure." To Lorre she said, "Why are you always late?"

He settled into a chair. "This time I ran into Lisa Schmidt. Don't give me such a look! I was very sweet to her and I apologized for last night and I invited her to go dancing tonight but she declined."

"Very wise of her."

"Don't be unkind, Greta. Am I to understand you're inviting me to lunch?"

"It will save time, so let's get to work." She reached for her script on the dressing table.

Lottie passed around a tray of appetizers. "Your favorite," she said, terribly pleased with herself, "skinless and boneless sardines on buttered toasted wheat bread."

Garbo popped one into her mouth and the look of pleasure on her face reminded Mercedes of an advertising logo for a milk company's Elsie the Cow. Garbo asked Lorre, "Do you like the revisions?"

"Very Brechtian."

"What does that mean?"

"What do you mean what does that mean?" retorted Lorre, bristling. "Have you never read Brecht?"

"Salka made me read something he wrote called *Mother Courage*. She wanted me to play it. I'm too young. It bored me."

"Brecht, as a writer, is a law unto himself. He's very sardonic, very bitter and very witty. I have a print of his movie version of *The Threepenny Opera*. He wrote that with Kurt Weill."

"Lotte Lenya's husband?" asked Mercedes.

"Yes," replied Lorre. "I'll run the movie for you if you like, Greta."

"Will it be instructive?" asked Greta.

"It will familiarize you with the man's work. On the other hand, it's very slow and a bit tiresome. It's better on stage. I was at the premiere in Berlin before I fled to England."

"Why haven't we met Brecht?" asked Garbo.

"You wouldn't want to," advised Lorre. "His teeth are worse then Henkel's, his breath is deadly and when he decides to bathe, they raise flags from half mast."

"Charming," said Mercedes. "But he's a damned good writer."

Lottie was whipping up individual omelets. The odor was intoxicating. Lorre sniffed some cocaine and said, "Greta, let's get started. I always have trouble with lines on the first day of shooting."

"There's something else that's bothering you," the astute actress said.

"Oh no. Nothing. I didn't sleep very well last night." He lit a cigarette. There's plenty bothering me, he thought. My family trapped in Europe. Guiss's hold on me. And Lisa Schmidt. Who is she working for? Who?

Marion Davies and William Randolph Hearst were sitting across from each other on the second-floor veranda eating lunch. Her eyes were slightly bloodshot, a souvenir of some lonely, heavy drinking the previous night. She lifted a glass and drank.

"What's in that glass?" Hearst squeaked sternly. His voice was so abnormally high-pitched that whenever he spoke, people looked around in fear that there was a displaced rodent on the loose.

"Same thing that's in yours. Vichyssoise." She always drank vichyssoise from a glass. This one was heavily laced with gin. She held it out to him. "Want a sip?"

"I've got my own. What are you staring at?"

"There's two guys fiddling with the front door of that monstrosity next to us. Why don't you do something about having it torn down?"

"I have to own it before I can tear it down."

"So why don't you buy it?"

"Because I don't want it."

"Okay, then I'll buy it."

"No you won't."

"Yes I will. I've got plenty of cash of my own." She wondered if he'd found out she'd bought into the skyscraper on the southeast corner of Park Avenue and East Fifty-seventh Street in New York. She'd bought it in her sister's name.

"I don't want you wasting your money on unprofitable property."

"I don't want to profit from the damned monstrosity, I want to tear it down. By Christ, they're going into the house. Do you suppose they're planning to move in?" She made a move to shout at them, but they were already in the house, out of sight, out of earshot.

Inside the house, Herbert Villon said to Arnold Lake, "We should have brought swimsuits and taken advantage of the weather."

"We should have brought gas masks." A noxious odor permeated the place. Arnold signaled Villon to open the windows. This Villon did with difficulty. The window seams were warped and misaligned from lack of use. The front door led into a huge living room seemingly furnished and decorated in early Caligula. Arnold pried into sideboards and end tables while Villon nosed into closets and behind pieces of furniture. There was nothing to interest them. Arnold opened a door at the far side of the room. "Hey, the library."

"Oh goody," said Villon, trying desperately to ward off suffocation, "let's hope there's a wall safe. I love cracking wall safes, especially if they're hidden behind a framed print."

There were no books in the library. There was a big desk and an assortment of furniture that defied description. Nothing matched. Villon gurgled happily when he found the wall safe behind a poorly framed print of "Whistler's Mother." While Arnold rummaged about in the desk drawers, Villon worked on cracking the safe. Over his shoulder he asked Arnold, "Find anything?"

"So far a dog-eared paperback of the collected works of Schiller . . ."

". . . Whoever that is . . ."

". . . Some grocery receipts, a rotted half-eaten pear . . ."

". . . Somebody was a slob . . ."

". . . A dead roach . . . rigor mortis must have set in weeks ago . . ." He opened the last drawer, ". . . a jock strap . . ."

". . . In a desk drawer of all places?"

"Somebody was a lousy housekeeper or had a perverted sense of humor. Where the hell is that stench coming from?"

"Maybe from the cellar."

"The house doesn't have a cellar."

"Maybe from the attic."

"No attic either."

"Well somebody was a cheapskate. Voilà!" The safe door swung open. Arnold joined him at the safe. Villon murmured, "Just like Old Mother Hubbard. When she got there, the cupboard was bare." He moved away from the safe with disappointment. He crossed to a door and opened it. "I have found the kitchen."

"Chalk one up for you." They entered the kitchen and attacked the cupboards and the refrigerator. "Cheap dishes, dime-store pots and pans, cutlery handed down from some forgotten dynasty . . ." Arnold continued the inventory, to include frayed dishcloths, tasteless tablecloths and napkins, while Villon examined the interior of the refrigerator.

"It's just as discouraging in here," said Villon. "Some old piece of what might have been cheddar, a half-empty jar of peanut butter, likewise apple jelly, some blob on a dish that defies description and I'm not up to the challenge . . ."

Arnold said with disgust, "Whoever these Wolheims were, Mrs. Wolheim was a lousy housekeeper." He opened a door. "This is a pantry. Do you hunger to examine the pantry?"

"Well as long as we're here, it shouldn't be a total loss." They entered the pantry. It did not elevate their spirits. It also revealed nothing of importance or interest other than a shelf that held several brands of laxatives. Villon commented, "Somebody has problems." The door next to the pantry led outside to an enclosed garden. There they saw a marble birdbath, a variety of garden furniture that ranged from wicker to iron grillwork, and what looked like the remains of either a dog or a coyote.

Arnold asked, "Are coyotes known to come down from the hills and invade the beach?"

"Only when they're longing for a dip." Villon led them back into the house. "The animal isn't the reason for the smell. It must be upstairs. I better warn you in case you're unfamiliar with the odor. There's every probability there's a corpse up there."

"Oh please. Not before lunch."

They found her in what they assumed was the master bedroom. She was laid out on the bed, her eyes open with what was either fear, horror or just plain old-fashioned surprise. Villon studied the corpse while a nauseated Arnold forced windows open. Villon said, "She was probably in her fifties. Just about five feet in height, very very plump and she mistreated her hair. It's sort of a dung-brown color. She's wearing a thin, very cheap wedding ring and the wristwatch is a Farber."

"German make," said Arnold, who reluctantly joined Villon at the bed.

"I don't know why I'm thinking this is probably Mrs. Wolheim."

"She looks like a forgotten German potato dumpling. Do you suppose with any luck that phone works?"

The phone was on an end table on the opposite side of the bed. Arnold lifted the receiver, listened and smiled. "Allah is good. The operator to get your team?"

Villon took the phone from him. "That would be very naughty. This is Santa Monica's territory. But I'm feeling very wicked today. This stench is causing my senses to reel." He called his precinct and requested a photographer, a forensic team and the coroner.

"What will you do if the Santa Monica cops turn up before your boys get here?"

"I'll feign amnesia."

"Say Willie." Marion Davies was at the railing of her veranda, now wearing a sailor hat and carrying in her right hand a glass of cold *scharv* laced with a healthy infusion of vodka.

"What, honey?" he tweeted while trying to read Louella Parsons's column.

"There's something going on at that house. For chrissakes will you come over here and look? You're supposed to be a newspaperman, aren't you curious? Those cars are unmarked but if them ain't cops swarming into the place then Greer Garson's my mother."

Hearst stood behind her, saw a number of men get out of a Ford and a Chevrolet and enter the house. "Well," he finally said, "that certainly looks like it might be police activity."

"Well it sure ain't a meeting of the local B'nai B'rith."

Hearst left her and went inside to phone his managing editor. Marion went to her bedroom to use her private phone. She called the Goldwyn Studios and asked to be put through to Greta Garbo's dressing room.

Lottie Lynton took the call. "Oh hello, Miss Davies. Miss Garbo is on the set. I don't know how long she'll be. It's the first day, you know, and everyone's nerves are on edge. Mr. von Stroheim slapped an extra who punched him in the jaw, you know, little incidents like that . . . but wait . . . wait . . . here she is. . . ."

Garbo came storming through the doorway, a dangerous tornado. "That son of a bitch. That hideous Hun. How dare he tell me how to play comedy. His idea of hilarious is dissecting a cat while it's still alive!"

Lottie had her hand discreetly across the mouthpiece of the phone. "I have Miss Davies here."

"I can't talk to anyone now. I'm too upset."

Lottie repeated Garbo's words efficiently. Then she listened and, eyes wide with excitement, reported, "She says . . . er . . . the place is swarming with the fuzz . . ."

"Fuzz? What fuzz?" Garbo was lighting a cigarette and puffing it ferociously.

"The police!"

"What place? What are you talking about?"

"Where the Wolheims lived!"

Intrigue quickly replaced anger. Garbo took the phone and asked, "Marion? What's going on?"

She heard Davies saying, "I saw two guys go in there about an hour ago. Then all of a sudden a couple of cars show up . . ." In the distance she could hear the wail of an ambulance siren. ". . . With what certainly were more cops, plainclothes guys, and one carrying a little black satchel so he had to be the sawbones . . . you know . . . um . . . uh yeah . . . the coroner. So they've probably found a stiff in the joint." Marion was enjoying herself immensely. "How about that! Murder right next door! Oh Christ, Willie's phoning his editor and that means reporters and photographers and they'll be questioning me and I look like shit warmed over! Ethel! Ethel!" she shouted for her maid, "Come in here and make me look young! There's going to be photographers! Greta? I'll keep you posted!"

Marion Davies slammed the phone down and hurried into the room she'd had refitted as a beauty parlor. Ethel had preceded her and was mixing magic potions in pharmacy bowls. "And get the clamps to pull my skin back behind my head. I'll wear a gold brocade turban, that'll hide them." She shouted at another maid who had entered the room. "Get over to the house next door and try and find out who was murdered." The ambulance had arrived and the shrieking siren was abruptly choked off. "The meat wagon's here! I haven't been so excited since I got screwed by Charlie Chaplin!"

The police photographer photographed the corpse from every angle while the forensic team went to work on the room. The coroner, with a practiced eye, took one look at the texture of the dead woman's skin and said she'd probably been dead anywhere from five days to a week.

"Any idea what killed her?" asked Villon while Arnold Lake stood next to him, hands in his pockets, foreseeing that the woman's murder would soon lead to a large-scale explosion of international intrigue. If she was the putative Mrs. Wolheim, and if the Wolheims were German agents, then her murder could possibly trigger a string of killings confined to the family of agents.

He heard the coroner saying, "If you'll look at her head, you'll notice there are patches on the skull where she's lost clumps of hair." He cleared his throat. "There are certain blood disorders that can cause that. But in this case, I'll put my money on thallium nitrate. That's a highly toxic metal." They stood to one side as the meat wagon orderlies entered with a stretcher and prepared to remove the body. "It's rarely used in one dose. It's usually served a little at a time, like cyanide, so it takes the victim a few weeks to die. The symptoms, in addition to the loss of hair, include a painful burning in the feet. I'll know more when I've cut into her." He watched the corpse being carried out of the room and then said to Villon admonishingly, "Herbie, aren't you being a bad boy? Doesn't she belong to the Santa Monica boys?"

Villon said with an innocent look, "Finders keepers."

At the studio, Martin Gruber made it his business to encounter Lisa Schmidt on the set. "Ah Miss Schmidt. Just the person I've been looking for."

"Mr. Gruber? How can I help you?"

He walked her out of earshot of the personnel setting up for the next scene. "Guiss has ordered me to find out everything I can about you."

"So he's still suspicious?"

"He's tenacious. And very thorough. So I thought we might meet and concoct a biography for you that will satisfy all of us. Nothing too outrageous, mind you. But something that will tell him something but will really tell him nothing. And then he'll be satisfied and compliment me for a job well done. He might even give me a raise."

"Shall we meet and do it together? What do you suggest?"

"Why don't I draw up a rough treatment, and then you can add or subtract or embellish. You're twenty-four, right?"

"Right."

"Orphaned early in life and raised by a cruel spinster aunt?"

"No, it was actually a cruel maternal grandmother who claimed I was illegitimate."

"That bothered you?"

"Oh not at all. I remember mother used to introduce me to a wide variety of uncles at breakfast frequently. They came in all shapes and sizes and a variety of denominations and I adored almost all of them, especially the ones who'd give me some money if I'd let them cop a feel. All kidding aside, I was born in Cleveland, my parents were Bavarian immigrants, and they were killed in a train crash about three years ago."

Gruber thought for a moment. "Nah, too mundane. Let me work on it and I'll soon have a rough draft for you."

In an exaggeratedly loud voice she said, "I'll have those notes typed up for Mr. Guiss, Mr. Gruber. I'll get to it immediately."

Von Stroheim had come upon them unseen by Gruber. "What notes?" he growled.

Gruber took over. "Mr. Guiss wants a daily progress report."

The director's eyes narrowed. "Why?"

"Why, to know how you're progressing. Isn't it usual for the director's assistant to keep a daily report on how many minutes have been filmed each day?"

Von Stroheim's skin turned purple with rage as he exploded, "I will not be persecuted! We have only just begun shooting today and already the vultures are gathering to plague me!"

"Please, Mr. von Stroheim," placated Gruber.

The director shouted, "If you wish to please Mr. von Stroheim you'll keep to hell away from my kingdom! This set is my kingdom! I am the absolute ruler. If Mr. Guiss wants a daily progress report, tell him it cannot be provided with any degree of accuracy because from one day to the next I'm never sure what I have accomplished until I have studied the rushes and decided what is usable and what needs to be reshot and I am a *very slow study!* Now get the hell out of here!"

Gruber fled.

Von Stroheim took Lisa by the arm and hustled her to one side. "What's going on between you and Peter Lorre?"

She felt the blood draining from her face. "Nothing," she managed to say.

"He's very upset. He's giving a very poor performance. I'm told there was a confrontation with you last night that led to circumstances that have left him upset and nervous and unhappy, and I will not tolerate that."

Lisa told him about the previous evening's confrontation and then Lorre's apology earlier that afternoon. "That's all it was," she said in conclusion, "an innocent case of mistaken identity."

Von Stroheim was just about her height, about five feet four or five. They were standing almost nose to nose. "Tell me the truth, young woman. Are you involved in an undercover activity? Are you a spy for Hedda Hopper?"

She collapsed with laughter and von Stroheim smiled. She's a good girl, he thought, a very good girl. I must lure her to a nondescript motel in Laguna Beach and ravage her.

Twelve

When it seemed a small war was about to erupt between Herb Villon and the Santa Monica Police Department, Arnold Lake arranged for his superiors to come to Villon's assistance, which resulted in an uneasy truce. The Santa Monica police smarted from the illegal invasion and threatened revenge.

William Randolph Hearst succeeded in scooping his rival newspapers and bought Marion a diamond tiara that would later be inside the bag of jewelry she gave him to pawn when his newspaper empire was tottering on the brink of bankruptcy.

When Garbo came home from the studio that night with Lottie Lynton, she found Herb Villon and Arnold Lake waiting for her in Villon's parked car. Villon apologized for the invasion of her privacy but since she and Salka Viertel were the only people he knew to have seen the Wolheims, it was possible she could make an identification, if the dead woman was indeed Mrs. Wolheim.

Wearily, Garbo said, "Come inside, gentlemen. Salka Viertel, my good friend, will be here any moment now. Perhaps she can assist in identifying the woman." Lottie took Garbo's coat and bustled out of the room to prepare drinks. Villon and Arnold watched Garbo cross to the couch and slink down onto it. This is the fabulous Garbo, thought Villon, here she is in the flesh, and she's even more beautiful and seductive then she is on the screen.

So this is Garbo, thought Arnold Lake. Big deal. Later, he would dine out on stories about his pal Greta until all of Washington, D.C., stopped inviting him to social events in hopes he would now have the time to find a new routine.

They heard Garbo say, "I'm sure Saloman also saw the Wolheims. He's one of my neighbors. A retired insurance broker. A widower. He lives alone." She indicated with a tired wave of a hand in which direction they might succeed in locating Mr. Saloman. "I'd phone and invite him here but I have never invited him here and I see no reason to upset a precedent. I assume you have a photo of the dead woman, so why not take it to Mr. Saloman, since Salka might be a while yet and I would like some time to pull myself together. The first day of a film is always very trying. You are working with actors mostly you have never worked with before, and you have to learn to accommodate yourself to so many of them. It's like being given a new and unfamiliar family, you understand?"

They understood. Villon volunteered to go see Saloman. Arnold stayed behind and eagerly took the scotch and soda Lottie brought him. Garbo just as eagerly sipped her vodka on the rocks and kicked her shoes off. She studied Arnold for awhile, her inquisitor eyes making him so uncomfortable, he thought she'd put Torquemada to shame. Finally she said, "You are a federal agent, you say?"

"Yes."

"A G-man."

"Yes."

"Like James Cagney?"

"He's not a G-man."

"He was one in a movie I saw years ago. He was a cute G-man. Are there other G-men who are cute?"

"We don't see ourselves as cute."

"I think you're cute." She grinned. "Don't take me seriously. After a day with Erich von Stroheim and Peter Lorre it is understandable that I'm feeling a bit quixotic." She paused and then said, "I should like to play that part."

He could barely keep up with the way her mind jumped about. "What part?"

"The character from which the word 'quixotic' evolved. Cervantes's Don Quixote. But the correct pronunciation is 'Kee-ho-tay.' See, you are surprised. Garbo is educated." She laughed. "Not really very much. I was a poor student. As I grew older, I learned and absorbed from others. That is why I am most frequently quiet. I am quiet because I am listening and learning. Ah! I hear Salka's car! Lottie! Mrs. Viertel is here! Bring her a dry sherry to compliment her dry wit." Garbo crossed to the door and Salka Viertel entered. Garbo introduced her to Arnold just as Herb Villon returned.

Salka liked both men at once. They were handsome and of the no-nonsense type she appreciated.

Villon told them, "Mr. Saloman gave me a positive identification."

"Yes?" Garbo's head was cocked to one side. "Show me the picture." It was in the manila envelope he was holding. She and Salka examined the photograph. Garbo grimaced. Salka said, "Yes that's the poor dumpy thing." Garbo agreed. Salka asked, "How was she killed?"

"The coroner has tentatively suggested the possibility of a toxic metallic poison called thallium nitrate. You'll notice she's missing patches of hair. That's one of the symptoms."

Garbo left them and walked to the window that overlooked the ocean. "Look, Salka, look! The dolphins are out there playing!"

Salka explained to the men, "She dotes on dolphins."

Lottie came from the kitchen with a tray of hors d'ouevres, and offered them to Garbo's guests. She smiled at Villon. Villon thought, I know this woman. I've met her before. But I can't remember. It'll come to me. It usually does.

"You have the weirdest look on your face, Herb."

He told Arnold that he thought he'd known Lottie at another time.

Arnold suggested, "Why don't you ask her. Did she look as though she recognized you?"

Villon couldn't answer because Garbo and Salka returned from their dolphin watching and began bombarding him with questions. Salka took the lead. "Was there any evidence in the house as to her real identity? Obviously Wolheim is a pseudonym."

Villon told them, "There was nothing. No purse, no identification whatsoever. The labels on her clothes were store-bought, cheap store-bought, downtown L.A., not easy to trace. Forensics have dusted the house but found nothing of any importance. A few fingerprints have been sent to D.C. for possible identification. The lab is examining some leftover peanut butter and apple jelly we found in the refrigerator for possible traces of the poison."

Salka asked with interest, "The refrigerator was connected? The electricity hadn't been disconnected?"

"And the phone was working," contributed Villon.

"Then you must investigate the utility companies and find out who pays the bills." Garbo was back in the spotlight again. "Well, shouldn't you?"

Villon was abashed. "Chalk one up for you, Miss Garbo. We should have thought of that ourselves."

"But the people who have paid the bills probably aren't real." She was stroking her chin. "Yes? I'm right? It's logical, yes? If the Wolheims were German agents, whoever paid the bills didn't use a real name. Oh my God!" Her hand flew to her mouth.

Alarmed, Salka cried, "What's wrong? Greta, what is it?"

"Kriegman!"

Arnold asked, "Who's Kriegman?"

"Guiss's butler. Lottie, I need more vodka." Garbo sat. "Earlier today, I was discussing the Wolheims in my dressing room with Peter Lorre and my friend Mercedes de Acosta. There had been some misunderstanding on Peter's side when he thought one of the girls who works with von Stroheim was a mysterious woman in need of rescue on our beach several weeks ago. Nice girl, Lisa Schmidt." Villon and Arnold refrained from exchanging glances. "Anyway, in discussing Mr. Wolheim, I had this feeling I had seen someone who resembled him, and then I remembered who that was. Kriegman!"

Again Arnold asked, "Who's Kriegman?"

"He's the butler who works for Albert Guiss!"

Now Villon and Arnold exchanged glances. Villon said, "We'll have to meet this butler Kriegman."

"I can phone Albert for you if you like," offered Garbo.

"Oh no no. We need the element of surprise here." Villon was adamant. "We'd prefer to drop in on Mr. Guiss by surprise."

Garbo sounded mournful. "Mr. Guiss is not easily dropped in on. He lives in a fortress in Bel Air equipped with very sophisticated electrical equipment to keep intruders out. I have been there several times. I know." Lottie brought her the vodka refill.

Suddenly Villon asked Lottie, "Excuse me. But have we met before?"

Lottie rewarded him with a lavish smile. "But of course we have. Almost ten years ago. You arrested me."

Garbo's mouth hung open. Salka said, "He *what?*"

"He arrested me," insisted Lottie. "And I'll never forget, he was terribly polite and very nice." She reminded Villon, "You had that blonde girlfriend of yours with you."

"Hazel Dickson."

"That's it. Hazel Dickson. She was a gossip writer or something."

"That's right."

"What's become of her? You dump her?"

"No. She joined the army. She's a WAC Captain."

"She ought to do right good at that."

"Right now she's having a bit of trouble keeping a lot of the girls serving under her from getting engaged to each other. Say, what's your name again?"

Her hands were on her hips with annoyance, as though *How dare he not remember her.* "Lottie Lynton, for crying out loud!"

"Lottie. . . ."

". . . *Lynton.*" She underlined her name with impatience. Salka, shaking her head in disbelief, went to the bar to refresh her sherry.

Garbo was delighted at the unexpected confrontation. "Lottie has been with me over two years now. Her parole officer entrusted me to her care. She belongs to me now. She's a treasure."

It was coming back to Villon. "You killed your husband."

"And how, the mean son of a bitch. I kept warning him to stop beating up on me. The damn fool called my bluff so I killed him. I still carry a lot of those scars."

"I remember now," said Villon. "You poisoned him."

"You got it!"

"It was something like cocoa, something like that, right?"

"It was hot chocolate," shrieked Garbo, unable to contain a sudden fit of laughter.

"That's right!" cried Villon. "Hot chocolate!"

Lottie stood tall and proud. Poisoning her husband would be a feat about which she would crow for the rest of her life.

"It was cyanide, right?" said Villon.

"Wrong." She folded her arms. "It was thallium nitrate!" Garbo's laughter died. Lottie couldn't understand the sudden silence. "Well that's what it was. I read up on it in a book of poisons I found in my local library. The poor bastard. It took weeks for him to die. And I had to listen to him yelling in agony, how his feet were on fire and then the clumps of hair began coming out when he combed himself and I tell you, watching him go just about took my appetite away. But he finally went and they caught up with me and I'm out on good behavior and here I am."

"Yes indeed," agreed Villon, "Here you are."

Thirteen

A few hours later over dinner at Musso and Frank's popular restaurant on Hollywood Boulevard, Villon still couldn't get over Lottie Lynton's brazen performance in Garbo's living room. "The way she carried on about poisoning her husband, you'd think she'd invented the safety pin. Have a potato pancake."

Arnold declined the offer. "Do you think she did in Mrs. Wolheim?"

"No motive. Why would she? Just to keep in practice?"

"Well, we have a thallium nitrate killer living in the vicinity of a thallium nitrate victim. How coincidental can a coincidence get?"

"Thallium nitrate's very popular. I had a case a couple of months ago involving some nut case who got rid of his wife, her mother and father, and three teenage children. He claimed God told him to do it."

"Which God?"

"In his case? Probably Buddha. The family was Chinese. They owned a restaurant."

Arnold speared a boiled carrot and was about to consign it to his mouth when he lowered the fork and said, "Martin Gruber."

"What about him?"

"The butler. Kriegman."

"Come on, man, make sense."

"Gruber can take a picture of Kriegman and get it to us. We've got a new camera that works sensationally indoors. They're sure to have one in the local office."

"Arnold, you're a genius."

"I'll get after it first thing in the morning."

"Supposing Gruber balks? He can't go chasing after Kriegman yelling 'Hey Kriegman baby, watch the birdie!' "

"He's clever. He's one of the best informants we've ever had. He comes from a long line of traitors. He didn't need much training when Lisa brought him to us."

"He's that good? You sure he isn't double-headed?"

Arnold gave it some thought. "Work for us and work for them? Anything's possible in this game." He shook his head. "No, not Gruber. He's given us too much stuff over the past year that's been pure gold. He's helped us crack two codes, he got us a great list of fifth columnists working in the country, and the Germans don't pay all that good. We pay *real* good."

"How long has he been in the Guiss camp?"

"Over a year now."

"And he still hasn't been able to nail Guiss and his satellites?"

"Herb, you're such an innocent. When we're out of this place, I'll tell you some bedtime stories."

"What's wrong with here?" asked Villon, while challenging a limp, overcooked asparagus spear.

"You never know who's in the next booth."

"I know who's in the next booth. A couple of French actresses, Fifi D'Orsay and Yola D'Avril. Nice girls."

"Are they Free French?"

"Don't know. I've had no call to make them an offer."

* * *

"I swear, herr Guiss, I swear I didn't kill her! The last I saw of her was over a week ago when she was packing to leave for Canada." Kriegman was dabbing at his damp forehead with a handkerchief. "It was arranged for our people in Toronto to get her back to Germany. Isn't that so, herr Henkel? You passed the message on to them."

In addition to Henkel, Risa Barron and Werner Lieb were in Guiss's office, all of them worried about what consequences might result from Mrs. Wolheim's murder. Henkel stifled a nervous yawn. "Yes, that is so. They didn't particularly want her back."

"Why is that?" asked Guiss.

"They had no further use for her back home. They would have preferred she stay here. They were arranging for her to work with a family in Boston, I believe their name was Kennedy. But Anna wanted to go home. She was frightened."

"Yes," bellowed Kriegman, "she was very frightened. She was gorging herself on peanut butter and apple jelly sandwiches when she wasn't wringing her hands and muttering 'Achtung, achtung' over and over again. And she was complaining how her feet were burning and she began losing her hair."

"Nerves," said Risa Barron flatly, "nothing but nerves. I had a sister who lost her eyebrows, her eyelashes and her pubic hairs when her husband left her for a houri in Morocco. Of course it all grew back later when she fell in love with a pharmacist. Nothing but nerves."

Kriegman was babbling away again. "You said yourself an agent is hopeless once they begin to lose their nerve. Perhaps if we had stayed on in that house, if you hadn't forced our disappearance after Pearl Harbor was bombed. . . ."

"Your usefulness in the house was finished. I needed you here, just as I needed the boys to join my armed guards." Guiss asked Risa, "The girl? Does she still dissatisfy you?"

Risa was busy fiddling with the clasp of a bracelet. "She tries hard. She's so ordinary. How did she get into undercover work? She's so plain, so ordinary. She should marry a butcher's assistant and have babies."

"She knows Mrs. Wolheim has been killed?"

"Of course she knows. She reads the newspapers."

"Did she say anything to you?"

"She said plenty to me. She's frightened. There were people who saw them on the beach when they took their nightly stroll, that Jew Saloman who lives next door to Greta. And Greta too, and her friend Salka Viertel. And I think Marion Davies when she and Hearst played tag on the beach. *Gott in Himmel!* We should send them all back to Germany and the sooner the better."

Kriegman paled. "Please! Don't send me back! I don't want to go back. There's nothing there for me."

"Oh shut up, you fool!" shouted Guiss. He got up and moved away from his desk, thinking aloud. "She was packed to leave for Germany. Was someone to escort her to the train?"

"I was," said Henkel. Then he smiled, "She was rather fond of me."

"Why didn't you take her to the train?"

"When I went to get her, she was gone. Nobody saw her leave."

"And nobody knows how she got back in the house."

"Her murderer knows." Risa Barron spoke sweetly, mellifluously. "Do you suppose the federals killed her? Do you suppose they murdered her and put her back in the house as a warning that they're on to us?"

Guiss said matter-of-factly, "When they're on to us, they'll come and get us."

Risa's eyes widened. "That prospect doesn't frighten you?"

"I don't frighten easily."

Werner Lieb asked, while polishing his monocle with a tissue paper, "Has it occurred to you that the murderer might be among us?"

"It most certainly has," said Guiss, "but who among us had a reason to kill her?"

"Do all murderers have to have a motive?" asked Lieb. "Aren't there killers who kill just for the thrill of killing? She was of no further use to the cause, right? Therefore, she was expendable."

Risa leaned forward in her seat. "You make it sound so plausible. Maybe you're the one who killed her."

"I'm a pragmatist, Risa. I think the investigation should be left in the hands of the police. The newspapers don't say how she was murdered, just that the body of a woman known as Mrs. Wolheim was found in a bedroom of a Santa Monica beach house in the vicinity of the homes of some very important celebrities. Hearst himself scooped his rivals. I think we should be more concerned with the poor showing on the part of our artists on the first day of shooting. Von Stroheim managed less than two minutes of usable footage. That's very bad."

"From what I saw of the first scene with Garbo and Lorre," contributed Risa, "their performances look very disappointing."

"They will improve," said Guiss with confidence, "and von Stroheim promises to get the lead out. They're all nervous. A first day, they tell me, is never easy."

"That's right," said Risa with a wicked grin, "it's like the first night of a honeymoon. All clumsy fumbling."

Guiss lit a cigarette. "We'll see what we've got when we view the rushes tomorrow. Maybe Greta won't sound good, but she'll certainly look good. Her color tests were remarkable." He smiled at the recollection. "How I would love to make love to her."

For the first time since she'd met Guiss, Risa felt sorry for him. Deep in his thoughts of the elusive Garbo, Guiss looked like a sad and vulnerable schoolboy.

On their way to Arnold's bungalow to continue their discussion of Guiss and company, Arnold and Villon paused in the Garden of Allah's busy bar for a drink. It was crowded with celebrities and Herb Villon was a sucker for important names. Dorothy Parker was sitting at a table with her husband, Alan Campbell, and the comedian Charles Butterworth. They heard Butterworth asking Mrs. Parker, "Have you read Steinbeck's new book?"

"Some of it."

"What's it like?"

She replied, "I've found more substance in tea leaves."

From another table writer-director Preston Sturges was having drinks with actor-humorist Robert Benchley. Benchley was discussing an actor Sturges was considering for his upcoming movie. "I think he's rather mediocre," Benchley said.

Sturges replied with a thick tongue, "He's not talented enough to be mediocre."

At the bar, actress Miriam Hopkins was trying not to look bored with her companion, actor Vince Barnett, who said to her from out of the blue, "Y'know Miriam, I think I lived in another life."

She said brightly, "Where you swung by your tail?"

Arnold nudged Villon. "Let's go to my bungalow. I've had it in here."

In his bungalow, Arnold removed his jacket and poured drinks for them. Villon settled into an easy chair and lit a cigarette. Arnold said, "You know what I think, Herb? I think the lady was done in by one of her own bunch."

"I think you may be right."

"I have to be right. As far as we know, she was just part of her phony family. She probably didn't know anybody else in L.A."

"What bugs me," said Villon, "is where was she holed up from the time she left the beach house December eighth until her murder? That's two months at least."

"They probably had her stashed in one of their safe houses. They've got at least three that we know of in the area." Arnold thought for a moment. "Somebody must have thought she was a threat or else she was of no further use to them and it was simpler to kill her than send her back to Germany. They have a route back through Canada, you know."

"So I've heard. Our friendly neighbors to the north realize how hospitable they're being to the Nazis?"

"They know, trust me, they know."

"Okay, now what about Guiss and his playmates?"

"We know," said Arnold, "that Guiss is Viennese and that he served as a lancer in the Viennese army. In that period he showed an amazing talent for diplomacy and won the friendship and admiration of some very powerful people. Now that's about twenty years ago. It's reasonable to suppose he was a war hero but I doubt we'll ever get the opportunity to see and admire his decorations. Then there's a five-year lapse and when he re-emerges, he is a very very wealthy man enveloped in a cloak of mystery."

"No wife? No children?"

"No nothing. Lots of rumors of mistresses. Risa Barron has been filling that bill for the last couple of years. He's showered her with a fortune in jewelry."

"What about Barron? Have you ever met her?"

"I've only seen photographs, newsreels: She's an ugly broad who's learned how to look good. Her features are all wrong but put them all together the way she does and you have what the pulp writers call a fascinating adventuress. She's played footsie with a lot of bad boys. Hitler and his gang, Mussolini and his pasta patrol. It's rumored she served time in a harem and came away with the title to an oil well. She was really nuts about Guiss but I hear there's the suspicion that it might be cooling. He's after Garbo."

"I'll bet he doesn't get her," said Villon.

"Then there's Werner Lieb. Everything about him is phony. His name, his monocle, his position as co-producer of the movie. What he is is Guiss's aide-de-camp. Guiss picked him up in South America about ten years ago where he was on the lam from Germany on a swindling deal. He took money from old ladies."

"So do department stores."

"There was also a charge of pederasty. Guiss cleaned his slate for him. He recognized in Lieb the kind of toady who wouldn't go bad on him. Guiss is very fond of him and Lieb is smart enough to know he'll never do better then he's doing now."

"And Henkel? What's his story?"

"He used to be an accountant. He tried writing short stories but never sold any, at least not to our knowledge. We don't think he's German. How's your drink?"

"It's fine. Tell me more. I'm fascinated."

"We doubt Henkel's his real name. The boys have studied his photographs and suspect he's a Slav, or a Pole, or even a Latvian. There's a candid shot of him grinning at some bathing beauty pageant and God Almighty those teeth of his look like they've been bombarded with buckshot."

"And then there's our boy Gruber. Mustn't forget to get that camera to him."

"There's also our girl Greta."

Villon sat up. "You're certainly not suspecting her of killing Mrs. Wolheim."

"Oh no way. But she spent time in Germany. She knew a lot of people there who today are active Nazis."

"So what? Pola Negri's back in town trying to make a comeback, remember her?"

"Silent pictures?"

"Right," said Villon. "But do you know where she was before the war broke out in Europe? She was in Germany starring in pictures for our boy Goebbels. Does anybody put her in a hot seat and grill her?"

"We've got a complete dossier on her. She's harmless. She worked in Germany because it was the only offer she had on the burner and she was running out of jewels to hock."

"You can't tell me Garbo might be a sympathizer. She was pretty damned smart tonight. 'Check out who's paying for the utilities!' Why didn't *we* think of that?"

Arnold shrugged. He was tired. He wished Lisa Schmidt would check in. He would need her to get the camera to Gruber. He wished he didn't feel so uneasy about her safety. There wasn't a fascist fanatic he knew about who didn't operate with a short fuse. Today it's "Don't kill her" and tomorrow it could be "What, she's still alive?" These people frightened him. They weren't human the way he'd been taught about humanity in Sunday school. They weren't real. He said it aloud and startled Villon. "Guiss isn't real!"

"What the hell is that supposed to mean?"

"I just had a hunch. There's something about Guiss that makes me suspect he's a fake."

"You mean he isn't really rich?"

"I mean, maybe it's not his money."

Villon was helping himself to another drink. "I know what you're getting at and it's an interesting premise. He was planned and created a billionaire, a mystery man. To act as a go-between. The mobs used to do that back in the twenties. Did you know they created George Raft and paid to make him a star just to get a foot inside Hollywood? Did you know that?"

"He's still a star, isn't he?"

"Go figure that one out. No talent and his name is still above the title."

"Figuratively, so's Guiss's. But what's his talent? Why has he been told to pour five million dollars into a turkey about Joan of Arc? Why is it costing five million? Lisa Schmidt says the sets aren't inexpensive, but they're not lavish. Outside of Garbo's million, the other members of the cast are working for their usual fees, nothing out of the ordinary there. She thinks maybe two or two and a half million would more than cover the cost of the production. So who's pocketing the difference?"

The phone rang. It was Lisa Schmidt. Arnold told her about the camera ploy and she assured him it would be no problem getting it to Gruber. She told him about Guiss ordering a thorough investigation into her background. Then they moved on to discuss the murder.

"Have you figured out how the body got into the house?" Lisa asked. "Was she still alive when she was in the house? Did she inconveniently die there and the killer decided he might just as well leave her there?"

"Good thought."

They discussed the utilities. Lisa said, "It's Guiss's property. Gruber told me that a long time ago. That's why the utilities are still connected. Why else did they have the meeting there? Why else were the Wolheims in residence for so long? I'll bet you a week's salary they had a shortwave sending and receiving set and were a relay station. Damn it, Arnold, it's in one of my reports that Guiss owns the house."

"I can't remember everything I read," Arnold snapped. "I get so many damned reports from J. Edgar I sometimes wonder when he finds time to hate so many people."

"I think it's a good chance one of her own people killed her. Maybe Guiss ordered it. If Kriegman really is Wolheim, maybe for one reason or another the lady was threatening to blow the whistle on the boys. Oh Christ I'm tired. I can't think. Let me know when you have the camera, we'll make arrangements to meet."

"What kind of a biography have you and Gruber cooked up for yourself?" asked Arnold.

"It's a beaut. Maybe we can sell the movie rights."

"Maybe. Get some sleep. Sorry I snapped at you. I'm a little punchy."

"We're all a little punchy. See you tomorrow."

"And Lisa, bolt your door and windows."

"I'm way ahead of you. I already have. It's very stuffy in here. Good night."

Villon poured another drink for himself and Arnold said, "You better go easy on that stuff. You'll have a bitch of a hangover in the morning."

"I never have hangovers. And I don't have an easy time falling asleep. The booze helps. I've got to work on this Guiss theory of yours. What did Lisa have to say?"

Arnold told him about Lisa's questioning if the woman was dead on arrival or conveniently expired there.

Villon said, "You're forgetting something. The poison was administered over a period of time. Somebody knew her favorite foods and laced them with the poison. I'll give you odds on that."

"Maybe peanut butter and apple jelly?"

Villon looked at his wristwatch. He knew the men in forensics would probably still be at it. It was only a little past ten. There were times when they conducted their experiments throughout the night, especially when they were facing an overload. He phoned his precinct and got through to one of the men in forensics. He advised him to test for thallium nitrate in the peanut butter and the apple jelly.

Jack Kelly of forensics told Villon, "That's just what we found. She must have eaten the stuff over a period of weeks, two, maybe less if she gorged on the stuff."

"Thanks, Jack." After he hung up, Villon said, "If she left the stuff behind in the refrigerator and doted on it that much, she had to get herself a fresh supply when she moved to the safe house."

"It was probably bought for her," said Arnold, "as a farewell gift."

Villon sighed. "Arnold, it's getting too late for irony. I'm going home. Could you point me to the door?"

Garbo sat in the darkness of her living room, puffing a cigarette, staring out at the ocean, watching the waves rise and crest against the shore, while harboring thoughts that until now had been strangers to her. Poison and murder and corpses in a neighboring house. Lottie Lynton and the joy she took in being a husband killer. Villon had identified himself as a detective, but what about the other man? His name, his name . . . she prodded her memory. Oh yes. Arnold Lake. Did he say he was a detective? No, he didn't. Then who is he? Still, he didn't have to say he was a detective, he was with the other one. They were quite chummy. They enjoyed each other. They worked well together.

Peter Lorre flashed into her mind. They hadn't worked well together today. Yes it was the first day and that old chestnut about the first day of a film being the most difficult always holds true and her nerves were genuine, but Peter's nervousness, she was convinced, was due to something else.

Fear.

Fear? But of what is he afraid? Could it be Lisa Schmidt? Could it be possible he really saw her on the beach that night? Right in his own home asking for help? Perhaps she never thought that someday she would confront him again. Peter was so positive at the studio that she was the woman in question, he was almost frantic about it. And then today, the very next day, he says he was mistaken. Yesterday's angry puppy is today's darling pussycat. And it's wrong.

She stubbed the cigarette out and went to the bar for a vodka on the rocks. With the glass in her hand, she opened the back door and went out to the patio. From where she stood, she could see the house of mystery. Bathed in the eerie glow cast by the full moon, it looked sinister and threatening. Mrs. Wolheim.

Mr. Wolheim. Kriegman. Now in the new guise of Guiss's butler. Does Guiss suspect that Kriegman is an enemy agent?

"Oh my God," she whispered, "I am so dense. I am so stupid. Of course he knows!"

She hurried back into the house, shut the door, drew the curtains to protect the blackout, and phoned Salka Viertel. Salka listened closely and absorbed the information and suspicions her friend was pouring out. Finally she said, "Listen to me, Greta. Whatever you suspect, you keep to yourself. It could be dangerous."

"When have I ever been afraid of danger? Didn't I co-star with John Barrymore?"

"Please Greta. If these people are what you think they are, and they suspect you know, your life could be in danger. God in heaven, it's already been in the papers we identified Mrs. Wolheim. So it stands to reason we'd also be able to identify *Mr.* Wolheim. And if it really is Kriegman, and he is now working for Guiss . . . oh my God Greta. We might at this very moment be marked women!"

"Stop being so melodramatic, Salka. You've written too many scripts. Who would dare kill Garbo?"

"Albert Guiss."

"You really think so? But how enchanting. This makes him a bit more interesting."

Salka said with irritation, "Stop talking like a fool. Maybe we should phone those detectives who came to the house. Maybe you should tell *them* what you suspect."

"Don't you think they are smart enough to have figured that out by themselves? They seemed quite intelligent. Oh Salka. How wonderful!"

"What's wonderful?"

"To be in danger! I don't think I have ever been in danger before. Oh Salka, it's a whole new emotion for me and I have been so desperately looking for something fresh in my barren life! I'm in danger! How marvelous! I'm tempted to phone Louella and Hedda but no, I will not. This emotion is mine, all mine, and I shall keep it to myself like the greedy, selfish little brat I am. I shall have another vodka and think about this. Go to sleep my darling. Go to sleep. We'll talk tomorrow." Gently, she replaced the phone on the receiver.

*   *   *

Go to sleep? Is she mad? Salka threw a pillow across the room and knew she was in for a restless night.

Garbo poured the vodka she had promised herself and then went back out on the patio. Did she think she had fooled Salka? Had she overplayed? Did Salka truly believe that Greta was not afraid of danger? The night air caused her to tremble. The night air? Or was it fear? God, you fool. Go back inside. Get off the patio. You're an easy target out here in the moonlight. She hurried back into the house. She latched the door securely. She hurried to her bedroom and came to a decision to share her suspicions with Villon and Arnold.

Fourteen

They were delighted she had phoned early that morning and asked them to come to the studio. Villon and Arnold sat with Garbo in her dressing room drinking hot chocolate catered by Lottie Lynton. Garbo wondered if they'd forgotten it was hot chocolate that had brought the curtain down on Mr. Lynton's life. Lottie also served a plate of Toll-House cookies she had baked early that morning. The men had nothing but admiration for the actress. Her deductions were intelligent and carefully thought out. Hers was a shrewd brain camouflaged by immortal beauty. They admired her and told her so.

Garbo clapped her hands with joy, a little girl winning the approval of her teachers. "And what is that interesting-looking camera you have there Mr. Lake?"

"Um, it's something I picked up in South America when I was down there a couple of months ago."

"It looks terribly sophisticated. I only have a little Brownie. Still, it takes very nice pictures. May I examine the camera?" Arnold handed it to her and she looked through the viewfinder and laughed. "You both look so serious. Is there film in it? I'd like to take your picture." Lake asked her not to and she pouted. "I take a very good picture, you can trust me. I have been taught by masters. Cecil Beaton, Louise Dahl Wolfe, Robert Capa who has gone off to photograph the war in Europe. But still, if you don't want your picture taken . . ." Her voice trailed off in childish disappointment as William Haines joined them. She introduced him to her visitors and then said to Haines, "You are out of sorts. What is wrong?"

"As Dr. Jekyll once said, I'm not myself today. Von Stroheim is in a bitch of a mood. He watched the rushes this morning with the wiener schnitzel gang and they were in an uproar." Haines grinned. "I knew he'd eff this movie up the way he effs up everything else. He shot thousands of feet yesterday and there's maybe a minute or so that's usable. You should have heard Guiss chewing him out. I almost felt sorry for Von but by God he gave as good as he got. He told Guiss where to put the rushes if he was that dissatisfied."

He treated them to a wicked impersonation of the director, strutting back and forth while slicing the air with an imaginary riding crop. "Who are you amateurs to tell me what looks good and what looks bad? You know nothing about judging rushes. Only the experienced eyes of the director and his editors know what can be used and what should be discarded. And sometimes even *we* miss a good shot and have to go back and run the rushes again and again until we have enough snippets that will piece together superbly. You have hired von Stroheim?" Haines puffed out his chest and stuck out his chin. "Then you must totally trust von Stroheim! I am not a hack like von Sternberg, who is finished in this business!" Garbo winced. She and Haines knew if it wasn't for this lucky throw of the dice, von Stroheim would be probably sitting in his agent's office listening to reason about returning to the front of the camera to portray any number of villainous Nazi roles now being offered him. Surely the man must recognize the industry was astonished that anyone would ever trust him with directing a movie again.

Haines continued his impersonation. "So if you want me out, I am out. Otherwise, go away and leave me to conduct the progress of the film. Greta is gorgeous and Lorre will improve . . ."

Greta squealed with delight. "Did he really say I was gorgeous? Oh Billy, how that pleases me. Then Lorre and I will be wonderful today. I'll grab Peter by the throat and make him give a performance. He broods too much about the mysterious woman on the beach."

Weirdly on cue, Lisa tapped at the door, which was wide open as Haines had left it, and joined them. "Good morning all." She said to Greta, "You'll be pleased to learn the monster thinks you look great in the rushes. I agree."

"You saw them?"

"Of course. I'm the director's assistant. I have to sit next to him with my notebook and translate his growls."

This amused Garbo. "Erich growls?"

"He provides a large variety of sound effects, few of them pleasant."

"You don't like him?"

"Oh I'm growing very fond of him." She was helping herself to coffee and accepted a cookie from Lottie Lynton. "He's growing on me. His insults are becoming melodious, and his complaints deserve a harp accompaniment." She took a bite of cookie and a sip of coffee. "All that bluster is a cover for his fear."

"But what is he afraid of?"

"Failure!" snapped Haines. He explained to Villon and Arnold, "Failure is the bubonic plague of Hollywood. Fail and you're out and the job offers decine and disappear and you're no longer needed as the extra man to complete somebody's dinner table arrangements, so you either take to drink or dope or both if you're not already hooked or else you go to Europe to look for a job, except these days there's a paucity of European want ads."

"Or you're very wise to turn to interior decorating and make a whole new career for yourself," Garbo said while smiling at Haines with admiration.

But Haines was now off on a tack of his own. "Or you're crazy enough to go into set decorating and spend the day dodging the slings and arrows of a demented martinet." He suddenly shrieked, *"Fuschia!"* Arnold's eyes widened at the outburst while Villon, with his eyes, caught Lisa's attention and subtly indicated the camera Arnold was holding. "The sunnuvabitch doesn't like fuschia! It reminds him of his mother's bedroom. How could a mother allow a son like that in her bedroom!"

Garbo reminded him mournfully, "But he was once an innocent little boy like you were."

Haines said haughtily. "I was never innocent. I was the smartest kid in the neighborhood. I slept with all the right people and got free ice cream and candy and didn't have to pay for my movie tickets. Oh the hell with it. I survived Louis B. Mayer, I'll survive Erich von Stroheim." He turned on Lisa. "I suppose he sent you here to find me?"

"No, he's busy excoriating Mr. Lorre. He's threatening to replace him with Donald O'Connor."

Garbo was horrified. "A teenage tap dancer as the Dauphin of France?"

"Why not?" asked Lisa, amused that Garbo would take von Stroheim's threat seriously. "Remember he tried to make a dramatic actress out of Fay Wray, but she ended up frustrating a big ape."

Haines asked from out of left field, "What's with that murder on the beach? Did you know the woman, Greta?"

"Only by sight. I assume you've read the papers. They say Salka and I recognized her. How tragic to die alone like that. But then, I shall also die alone, I think. Let us not dwell on death. We are surrounded by too much of it and it is inevitable and I am happy to be working again and I want to stay in a happy mood at least until I finish my scenes with Peter. They are supposed to be funny and I can't be funny if I'm not happy. And here's Alysia. Come in, Alysia. Am I needed on the set?"

Alysia Hoffman came in and Garbo realized there had been a dramatic change in the woman since the day Mercedes had introduced them to each other. She wore new clothes, simple but becoming. Where once her movements had been timid and tentative, she was now assured and straightforward. Garbo wondered if she had ever been a gym teacher before turning to acting. Alysia told her von Stroheim was still fussing with the camera setups.

Hearing the word "camera" reminded Arnold of their real mission to the studio. He heard Garbo introducing him and Villon to Alysia

Hoffman and wondered why her expression seemed to change when Garbo identified them as detectives. He wondered how Hoffman would react if he corrected Garbo and unmasked himself, albeit foolishly, as a government agent. Garbo further explained they were investigating the murder on the beach. Arnold asked matter-of-factly, "I don't suppose by some long arm of coincidence you might have known Mrs. Wolheim?"

"Me? How would I know her? You mean because I am also German?" She laughed and it was a very small laugh that could have used some energy. "We refugees don't all know each other. There are so many of us." Villon refrained from commenting "too many." "Anyway, since coming here, I have lived in a sort of self-enforced isolation caused by an economical situation. Now that has improved and I shall attempt to get out in the world a bit more, no?"

Lisa complimented her on the smart suit she was wearing. Alysia thanked her. Haines in his smart-aleck way asked the lawmen, "You guys got any hot leads?"

Villon folded his arms and said, "We're rounding up the usual suspects."

"Which is by way of telling me to mind my own damn business." Haines sighed and said to Greta with a finger to his cheek and with a little boy's voice, "Why is it the big boys don't want to play with me?"

Garbo ignored the question and told Villon and Arnold, "Alysia has been very kind in consenting to be my stand-in." Lisa admired Garbo for the generosity of the statement. Garbo continued, "In Europe she was a much bigger star then me."

"Oh no no," Alysia remonstrated, but not too strongly, thought Lisa.

"Oh yes yes. Alysia made pictures in all the major studios in Europe." Garbo ticked off the list and Villon and Arnold looked interested, though they were anxious to be alone with Lisa and get the camera to her without arousing suspicion. "It was being brought to Mexico for a film that sadly did not materialize that brought her to this end of the world. She had a hard time getting into America. Oh my heavens!" Her hands flew to her temples in a familiar Garbo gesture. "If I ever left the country now, they might not permit me to return!"

"Why not?" asked Villon.

"I'm not a citizen! I too am an alien!"

Villon asked, "Don't you want to become a citizen?"

"Oh yes. I should, shouldn't I? I've been here seventeen years, it's time I did something positive. I shall write to Eleanor Roosevelt and ask her to tell her husband to make me a citizen. You know," she began giggling, "she has sent me several fan letters. After seeing me as Camille, she asked for a lock of my hair." The giggle matured into a roar of laughter.

Arnold said through the din, "Mrs. Roosevelt asks for lots of locks of women's hair."

Garbo stopped laughing and raised an eyebrow. "Oh really? Well, now that you tell me this, I am no longer unique. Oh dear, how disappointing." Then she giggled again, "It wasn't my hair I sent her anyhow. I snipped off one of Freddie Bartholomew's curls and sent her that instead. Ha ha ha ha ha!"

Lisa Schmidt said, "I'd better get back to the set. If von Stroheim's missing me, he might blow a fuse."

Arnold interjected swiftly, "I don't suppose we could get a look at the set? I've never been in a movie studio before."

Lisa said, "But of course. Come with me."

Greta walked the three to the door. She said to Villon and Arnold, "You will keep me apprised of your progress?" Villon reveled in her conspiratorial tone of voice. "I feel so much a part of your case, now that I helped identify that poor woman."

"You'll certainly be hearing from us," Arnold assured her.

Alysia Hoffman mumbled something about probably being needed on the set too and followed the three out of the dressing room. Garbo said sadly, "They wouldn't let me take their picture."

Haines said, "Maybe they're on the lam?"

Garbo said indignantly, "Oh don't be so childish. What are you going to do about the fuschia?"

With hands on hips and a pout on his lips, he said, "I shall scrub the fuschia and shower the fucker with electric pink and with any luck it'll give him a deadly case of diarrhea." With a chuckle, he left.

Garbo was preoccupied with her own disturbing thoughts. Looking back on the previous half hour, she had the uneasy feeling the atmosphere had been charged with strange undercurrents. What was there about Arnold's camera that disturbed her? He said he had bought it in South America, but there was no manufacturer's identification to be seen anywhere. She had examined the camera carefully because cameras fascinated her, she had faced so many of them in the lifetime of her career. She demanded of her photographers complete and thorough details about how they were focusing on her and what were they trying to achieve. She had wanted to ask Arnold if it was possible to secure such a camera for herself, but she had a suspicion it was a make only an officer of the law could obtain. She knew cameras and that was a very special camera.

She accepted another cup of coffee from Lottie Lynton, who recognized the expression on Garbo's face and returned to the kitchenette, leaving Garbo to her thoughts. Garbo was now dwelling on Alysia Hoffman. Was Garbo crazy or had the woman seemed annoyed when Garbo was telling Villon and Arnold how famous Alysia had been and how she came into this country through Mexico?

Garbo was sitting at her dressing table and caught a glimpse of her dark expression. "Oh my, Greta! You must look happy. You must think happy. You have to play a happy scene! Did you hear what Lisa said, Lottie? I look wonderful in the rushes. I must phone Salka and Mercedes and tell them. Mercedes is a little cross with us today. She's jealous that we identified Mrs. Wolheim. Poor Mercedes. Perhaps she'll be lucky and find a murder victim of her own to identify."

Samuel Goldwyn said to Sophie Gang, "I'm grudging him but you have to hand it to von Stroheim. He's still an original." He had seen the morning's rushes from a clandestine position in the projection booth, his cigar smoke polluting it and nauseating the projectionist. "He's a master of composition. And that Greta, she's all by herself. There's nobody like her."

"I hear Peter Lorre's disappointing."

"He'll get better. Von Stroheim will show him the rushes and Lorre will be ashamed of himself and do better today. He's a wonderful actor. Here in Hollywood he's wasted. He should play Hamlet . . . ," he said, pronouncing it "omelet", "and maybe that king . . ."

"Lear?" asked Sophie.

"That's it, Lear. And also in that play about the *schwartzer* . . ."

"*Othello?*"

"Yeah, what I saw Paul Robeson play on Broadway. He should play the troublemaker . . ."

"Iago."

"Say listen, smarting pants, how do you know so much about Shakingspeares?"

"I majored in English literature in college."

"You went to college? I didn't know you're a college graduate. Well well well. So I really got a bargain when I hired you." He sounded as though he had just pulled off a big deal on Wall Street. "Anyway, Peter will improve. You should face it, for him, acting is like water off a dike's back."

It was all done so swiftly, no one noticed the progression of the camera from Arnold to Lisa and from Lisa to Martin Gruber. Gruber hurried away quickly, passing Alysia Hoffman as she returned to the set, ignoring her "Hello, Martin" in his anxiety to get to his office and secrete his contraband in the tote bag he'd brought with him to the studio. Strange, thought Alysia, he's never rude.

Fifteen minutes later, Gruber was in Guiss's office where the financier and his three associates were holding a council of war. Lieb was saying, "Perhaps we should admit von Stroheim is a mistake."

Guiss replied, "Don't be so quick to think of replacing him. We've only seen one day's work. Perhaps the man's right. We have to wait until he has more footage to work with, until he has what he calls the beginning of an assemblage. Then we'll be in a better position to judge what he's accomplishing."

Lieb insisted, "But look at all the waste! If that continues every day then the film will be vastly over budget and that must not happen."

Guiss exploded. Martin Gruber just jotted down notes, amused by the way these amateurs were at each other's throats already, and only a miniscule amount of footage in the can. Guiss shouted, "Since when have you become an authority on budgets? On a film you don't calculate money spent on a day-to-day basis, you have to wait a few weeks and *then* see where you are. Right, Henkel?"

"How should I know? This is my first movie."

Risa looked at him with undisguised revulsion. Guiss sometimes had incredibly strange tastes in associates. Where had her lover found this creature, she wondered. He was in residence long before her arrival and it was not easy to weasel information about himself out of him. He was as agile at evading answers as a farmer was crossing a field and avoiding piles of cow dung.

Guiss slammed a fist down on the desk. "I'm right and I will not be disagreed with!"

Ah, thought Gruber, he's already gone Hollywood.

Risa lit a cigarette, blew a smoke ring in Guiss's direction, and then said in a firm, strong voice, "Gentleman, we are avoiding a more pressing problem."

"And what is that?" asked Guiss, trying to control the trace of anger still left in his voice.

"Kriegman. What do we do about Kriegman? If Greta and Salka Viertel recognized Hannah Baum . . ." which was the name of the woman who had posed as Mrs. Wolheim ". . . surely Greta will have recognized Kriegman as having impersonated Mr. Wolheim."

Guiss was uneasy in his chair and finally crossed his legs. "She's seen him several times. She has said nothing."

"Perhaps she's playing a game," said Henkel. "She likes games, doesn't she?"

"She's a whiz at Chinese checkers," conceded Guiss.

"It's unfortunate it was she who had to be one of the group who recognized Hannah. That could pose a serious problem," said Risa.

"Meaning?" Guiss was obviously not happy with this conversation.

"Meaning sooner or later, if it already hasn't dawned on her, she will recall that Kriegman was indeed Wolheim. Those three oafs who posed as the sons are barely recognizable in those operetta costumes you have them wearing when they carry the spears, but again, there might come a time when she'll recognize *them*. And as for that tower of quivering jelly who is now my maid, Greta might realize at some point soon that *she* posed as the Wolheim daughter."

Guiss said, "Greta will not be coming to the house for a long long time. She had made it quite clear she doesn't accept social engagements when she is engaged in filming."

Risa commented sarcastically, "Such dedication to one's craft is only to be admired."

Werner Lieb said, "Miss Garbo has become dangerous. She is a threat to us and our assignment."

Guiss was lacing and unlacing his fingers. Martin Gruber cursed himself for perspiring. Guiss said, "Are you suggesting we consider eliminating her?"

Lieb said nothing. He watched Henkel stifling his perpetual nervous yawn.

"And what becomes of this project? What becomes of *Joan the Magnificent?*" asked Henkel.

Lieb said matter-of-factly, "If we play with fire, we'll get burned."

Guiss exploded again. "You damn fool! Murder Greta? Would you dare dynamite the Lincoln Memorial?"

"It's under consideration."

"*Dummkopf!* If Kriegman and the others are unmasked, it is simple to deny any knowledge of their background. Our story is that they were recently hired to augment my staff. How should I have suspected they are subversives? They came with excellent references and it is very difficult in these trying times to get competent household help, and so I was grateful to find them and hire them! Is that understood? And not another word about eliminating Greta, do you hear? Not another word!"

Henkel stifled another yawn.

Fifteen

It had taken courage and patience and cunning, but Martin Gruber got his picture of Kriegman. He happened upon him walking in the garden and in an agitated state, talking to himself. Gruber, unseen by Kriegman, positioned himself behind a privet hedge and got a succession of candid shots that, had Kriegman seen them, might have fired him with the ambition to become a professional model.

Gruber arranged to meet Lisa Schmidt to give her the roll of film. It had been agreed he was never to contact Arnold at the Garden of Allah or Villon at his precinct, for fear of being seen in either place and recognized by a German agent. As Arnold impressed on Gruber, they were all over the place. One of them was making a small fortune as a masseur to the stars and had developed a profitable sideline feeding items to the town's hungry gossip columnists.

Lisa dropped into the Garden of Allah for a drink the next evening, after leaving the studio, and found a seat at the bar next to Arnold Lake. As they chitchatted amiably, Lisa slipped the roll of film into Arnold's jacket pocket. After her third sidecar, Lisa was amenable to seeing the interior of Arnold's bungalow and so the evening was not a total loss for either one of them.

After the first day, the rushes improved considerably, and Peter Lorre was giving the kind of performance that made his fellow actors feel he was definitely a contender for an Academy Award nomination. They spoke of Garbo's work with awe, albeit reminding themselves that the Academy had never honored the actress and probably never would. Hollywood disapproved of mavericks. Mavericks made the Academy voter uneasy and uncomfortable.

Mercedes de Acosta was succeeding in making Greta Garbo uneasy and uncomfortable. Garbo managed successfully to camouflage her true feelings, asking her friend "So you think . . . how did you put it . . . I might be on the spot?"

"Now look Greta, it's quite obvious these Wolheims, or whatever the hell their names were, were answerable to higher authorities. And these authorities are undoubtedly fearsome and ruthless and dangerous. They'll stop at nothing to save themselves and they don't give a damn who they kill to protect themselves. Greta," she pronounced the name like a rumble of thunder, "I'm a Cuban and I have survived the overthrowing of power. My family fled Cuba because my father's life was in danger." Greta was thinking, Mercedes should have pursued an acting career. A little on the hammy side but she sure knows how to sell a point to the audience. "Greta," said Mercedes, with more thunder, even more fearsome, "we are none of us invincible. If you identified one member of that bogus family then they fear you can identify the rest of them."

"But I only know where Kriegman is. I don't know where the sons and the daughter are."

"Would you recognize them if you saw them?"

"I think so. Yes."

"Then you are *positively* dangerous to them. If Kriegman is working at Guiss's castle, how do you know the others aren't there too? You said yourself that the first time you went there for dinner there was a horde of extras and walk-ons working as guards, spear holders, maids, a large kitchen staff. Those four could have melted quite easily into that crowd."

"Yes," Garbo agreed, "anything is possible in Hollywood."

Lottie came out on the patio and announced Villon and Arnold. The sun was taking its own sweet time setting on the horizon and the moon was already struggling for position. Mercedes politely declined Lottie's offer of hot chocolate, although there was a chill in the air, and instead asked for a bourbon neat. Greta greeted her visitors and introduced them to Mercedes. As Lottie prepared and served drinks to the four of them, Garbo repeated Mercedes's apprehensions and suspicions.

Arnold said, "I can assure you they won't make an attempt on Miss Garbo's life. And as for the whereabouts of the so-called sons and daughter, we already suspect they're doing service in Guiss's place, but their only importance would be if one of them were a witness to the murder and that's highly improbable. Herb and I think Mrs. Wolheim was brought back to the house because the killer was getting impatient. She was taking too long to die. He felt the poison should have taken effect by then because she had gobbled such huge quantities of it. We think he took her to the house to finish her off."

Garbo suppressed a shudder. He was so cold and matter-of-fact in detailing this theory of the snuffing out of another human being's life. Whatever this Mrs. Wolheim had been, she had been a person and a person who died a horrible death and so, in Garbo's estimation, was worthy of some pity.

"So some days some guys get lucky," said Villon, taking over the narration from Arnold. "Once he got her in the house, probably complaining about her burning feet and her bouts of nausea, she suddenly collapsed, her eyeballs rolled up into her head, her skin turned grey and clammy . . ."

"Mr. Villon, please," pleaded Garbo.

"Sorry. I didn't mean to get so graphic." How he ached to hear her call him Herb. How he pined to call her Greta. How he wondered it would be like to caress and kiss her toe. He didn't care how big her feet were, these were the feet of Greta Garbo and if it was up to Herb Villon, they'd be declared a national treasure.

He heard Arnold say, "So he carried her to the master bedroom, laid her out and left her there."

"Where is her luggage?" Garbo had their attention. She smiled. "If she was supposed to be leaving the country, she would have to have luggage. Certainly a handbag. A passport?"

Arnold said, "You don't need a passport to board a submarine." To Garbo's inquisitive look he explained, "It's the usual transportation for getting their people in and out of North America. So Herb, where's the lady's luggage?"

"Either checked at Union Station or at a bus terminal. My guess is Union Station. Anyway, I'm ahead of you. I've got a couple of boys working on it."

Arnold fished an envelope from his inside jacket pocket. "And now Miss Garbo, would you please examine these?"

She took the envelope and found the pictures of Kriegman. "He's very photogenic, isn't he? In person he seemed so nondescript, but here he is, very imposing and very impressive. Obviously when these photos were taken he was in a state of agitation. But yes, this is Kriegman alias Mr. Wolheim. I'm sure even Kriegman is a false name." She stared at Mercedes. "Why are you so upset, Mercedes?"

"You're getting yourself in deeper and deeper! Is there no stopping you?"

"But Mercedes, I am not just Greta Garbo the actress. I am also Greta Garbo the soldier. I am serving my country. If Louella and Hedda knew, they'd stop writing those terrible lies about my lack of patriotism, but we don't dare tell them, do we gentlemen?"

"Certainly not those two," said Villon, and he thought of his Hazel Dickson soldiering for her country and wondering what she would have made of all this: him, Herb, sitting on a patio with Greta Garbo. It was as momentous to him as taking aim at Lincoln must have been to John Wilkes Booth.

"You're a damned fool," said Mercedes. "I need another bourbon." Lottie was called for and pressed into service. She had drawn the blackout curtains and they now sat in darkness, none of them inclined to move indoors.

Garbo told them the filming was finally accelerating, with von Stroheim giving it the pacing Guiss so desperately desired. Lorre's performance was now a vast improvement and she was feeling very good about her own. Then she asked the inevitable. "When do you plan to arrest Kriegman?"

"Why?" asked Villon.

"Because he's a spy!"

"We've got no proof."

"But I have identified him as Wolheim. And I'm sure so will Salka and Mr. Saloman."

"That's just identifying him as the man who passed himself off as a mysterious man named Wolheim. We don't know positively they were spies. We're very suspicious . . ."

"To say the least," interjected Arnold.

"But we haven't a shred of proof. Anyway, Miss Garbo . . ."

"Oh please, I'm Greta. We are working together. And you are Herb. And you are Arnold. After all, aren't we comrades in arms on the battlefield?"

Villon was aglow. Herb. Greta Garbo had pronounced his name aloud. Herb. It had a different sound, a different meaning. If his mother knew that her beloved Herbert had heard his name spoken by the glorious Greta Garbo, she would rise from her grave and materialize above them miming benedictions.

Arnold wondered why that stupid look on Herb Villon's face. He looked like Stan Laurel silently crowing about a major victory against Oliver Hardy.

Mercedes was speaking. "I don't see how you can minimize the threat of these people. They love to kill. I know, I was in Hamburg when that maniac was on the loose murdering at random, and he's still on the loose. Didn't any of you read about him? He was a poisoner. Oh my God, he wiped out a dinner party in a restaurant by tampering with their *spetzel.*" Herb thought, I wouldn't want my *spetzel* tampered with.

"Mercedes, are you suggesting this Hamburg poisoner has come all the way from Germany to poison sad Mrs. Wolheim?"

"Don't scoff, Greta. In this day and age anything is possible! Look at the success of Abbott and Costello!"

Garbo smiled. "They amuse me. 'Who's on first?' Ha ha ha ha ha."

"There's a fresh outbreak of killings in Dusseldorf," Arnold told them.

"How do you know this?" asked Garbo. How would he know what's going on inside Nazi Germany?

Arnold cleared his throat. "I happen to have access to certain information."

"Because you are a G-man?"

"You got it."

"Can I be a G-woman?"

"You have to be a graduate lawyer to join us."

Mercedes was doubly unhappy. A G-man, for crying out loud.

Herb was thinking Arnold should bite his tongue. Was it his fascination with the star that made him make the slip in front of the de Acosta woman, probably overheard by Lottie Lynton, or was it deliberate?

Garbo was asking Mercedes, "Where can I study law, Mercedes?"

Mercedes could no longer contain herself. She exploded. "You're talking like a god damned fool! You don't need to study law, you need a psychiatrist!"

Garbo said calmly, and with a trace of a smile, "I would only drive a psychiatrist insane. I visited one once a long time ago. He asked for my autograph." She explained to the others, "I never give autographs." She said to Arnold, "Wasn't the fact that you're a government agent supposed to be privileged information?"

Arnold said. "My superiors decided it was time to let the word out and make some people doubly uncomfortable."

"I wish you had let me in on that," said Villon.

"I was going to, but it was Greta who beat me to it by giving the game away."

"Oh my God," she gasped, "so I did! Forgive me, please forgive me."

Is this genuine or is this an act? Villon wondered. He heard Arnold assuaging Garbo and caught the look of confusion on de Acosta's face.

Garbo slapped her knee. "Aha!" She was pointing a finger at Arnold. "You want your true identity to become known to Guiss and his people. You led me into the slip of my tongue! By saying you have ways of knowing what's going on inside Germany. You knew my curiosity would get you to . . . ," she screwed up her face searching for the correct expression, ". . . to . . . to . . . I have it . . . blow your cover." She looked at them triumphantly. "So this is what it is to have your cover blown! It must be an exciting experience. But wait!" She was on her feet and pacing, circling them like a lioness about to pounce on her prey. "This is why the Wolheims were removed from the house, for fear that they might blow their cover. Then they actually were considered dangerous! They were afraid for their safety, my God, for their lives." She spun on Arnold. "Don't they execute spies in wartime? Oh poor Mrs. Wolheim. She didn't want to die. She wanted to go home and be a *hausfrau* again. She didn't want to be caught and executed. And I'm sure she didn't want to be poisoned. Arnold? Do you think she knew she was being slowly murdered? The burning feet, the nausea. Do you think she recognized she was being cruelly put to death? Oh the poor woman. I wonder if she is survived by children."

"Consider this, Greta," said Arnold. "Consider that in the course of her assignments, Mrs. Wolheim might have caused a number of deaths herself. She might have passed on information that sank ships and caused the destruction of ammunition factories or landing fields, she might have caused the deaths of thousands of soldiers and sailors."

"Oh what a terrible woman! Let's go inside. It's so dark out here I can't tell who is who. Lottie! Turn off the lights in the living room. We're coming in!"

"Are you going out?" Lieb asked Martin Gruber, who was carrying the tote bag that contained Arnold's camera.

"Yes, I have a dinner date. Mr. Guiss doesn't need me tonight."

"What a good-looking carryall. Did you buy it here in L.A.?"

"Yes. I found it in a shop on Beverly Boulevard."

Lieb reached for the bag. "It has an interesting pattern. May I take a closer look?" Gruber relinquished the bag. Lieb held it up, making a meal of presumably admiring the pattern. "Oh how clumsy I am." He had dropped the tote. The camera spilled out. "Oh my, I hope I haven't damaged the camera." He made a swipe at it and grabbed it before Gruber could retrieve it. Lieb examined the camera closely. "Very interesting. What make is this?"

"I think it's South American," said Gruber. "It's not mine. It belongs to a friend. I borrowed it to shoot some photos on the set."

Lieb screwed his monocle into his eye. "It takes pictures indoors?"

"Only when there is sufficient light, and the sets are brilliantly lit."

"How interesting. I should like to see some of these photos."

"They're being developed now. When they're ready, I'll show them to you." Damn, thought Gruber, damn this man. Now I have to hold on to the camera and do some shooting on the set. "I must go now, herr Lieb. . . ."

"*Mr.* Lieb. Don't make that slip again. Why are you so nervous? Why are you perspiring?"

"I'm going to be late. I don't like being late."

"I'm sorry if I detained you. Don't keep your lady waiting."

Gruber found a slight laugh. "Did I say I was meeting a lady?"

"Oh, I assumed you were meeting Lisa Schmidt. You seem so chummy at the studio."

"That's because we're working together. We have no other interest in each other, I can assure you."

"Why do you have to assure me?" asked Lieb coldly. "Your private life is your own business. I just happened to make a comment, that's all." He smiled, a thin, icy smile. "She's very beautiful. I wouldn't blame you if you were trying to make out with her. I wouldn't mind a taste of honey myself. Goodnight, Gruber." He dismissed Gruber abruptly and left the downstairs hall where they had run into each other.

Gruber hurried out of the house and found his car. Once behind the wheel, the tote bag placed at his side, he gripped the wheel tightly and waited for the panic to subside. Then he had the feeling he was being watched. He relaxed his grip on the wheel and turned on the ignition. From the corner of an eye he could have sworn someone at a window had pulled back a curtain slightly and was watching him. He pulled out into the road that led to the iron gates, perspiration dripping down his face. Perhaps it was nothing, he hoped, perhaps I'm getting paranoid. Perhaps Werner Lieb is smarter than we think he is. Perhaps he guessed the camera was a very special camera. I must go to the studio tonight with Lisa and photograph the set. God damn the man! *Mr.* Lieb. Not *herr* Lieb. He suddenly felt giddy. Oh well, what the hell. Herr today, gone tomorrow.

Lisa Schmidt wasn't happy about Gruber's encounter with Lieb and she knew Arnold and Villon wouldn't be either. She was even less happy about returning to the studio with Gruber and having to sign in with the guard on duty at the gate. Oh well, she'd concoct some excuse for their having to return after the others had gone. Fortunately, night shooting wasn't scheduled until the following week. It was now seven o'clock. Von Stroheim had called it a day shortly before six. He wanted to spend a few hours with his editors. He was probably closeted in an editing room with them now, preparing the next morning's rushes. After the first unpleasantness with Guiss, he now made a point of editing the rushes down to a reasonable length and carefully excising his excesses. He didn't want to lose this movie. He needed the quarter of a million he'd been guaranteed. He was heavily in debt. He needed to make money and start saving. The war wouldn't last forever. If this was his ultimate directing job, then he'd have to go back to playing Nazi villains. And when the war was over, such parts would be redundant.

This was the first time von Stroheim had taken her into his confidence. She sympathized with him. She wanted him to come up with a winner. But there was something she knew that von Stroheim didn't know and she was not about to share this ugly confidence with him. Arnold Lake's superiors suspected the film would never be completed.

Sixteen

Promptly at eight P.M., Guiss entered the dining room. There was no one seated at the table. The majordomo who oversaw the dining room greeted him with a warm smile and pulled back his chair at the head of the table, expecting Guiss to sit and be served.

But Guiss was perplexed and annoyed. "Where are the others?"

"I don't know, sir. I'm sure they're on their way."

"Where is Kriegman?"

"I don't know, sir. I have been in the kitchen the past three hours. I've seen no one but the staff there."

Abruptly, Guiss turned and left the dining room. The majordomo said something nasty and pushed the chair back into place. He looked at the serving table groaning under the weight of trivets and chafing dishes and serving plates covered to keep the heat in, an overabundance of food that could feed the starving people of Europe and leave some over for a nosh tomorrow. He had a feeling no one would arrive to eat this sumptuous dinner.

Guiss had buttonholed Risa Barron's maid, Agathe, who had impersonated the Wolheim daughter. Her hands fluttered like the wings of a frightened butterfly expecting to be pinned and exhibited under glass. "She didn't tell me where she was going. She put on her diamond and ruby bracelets and her amethyst necklace and, dragging her sable on the floor behind her, she left her suite saying she needed to be by herself tonight."

"And Henkel? And Lieb? Do you know where they are?"

"If they're not here, sir, then they're gone, sir."

"And Kriegman? What has become of Kriegman?"

Fear had dampened the palms of her hands and she was trying to dry them by rubbing them on her apron. "I haven't seen him in several hours, sir. He . . . he's been acting and talking very strangely, sir. He . . . he's frightened. Ever since Hannah was found murdered, he's been frightened. Oh sir," she blurted out as tears sprang to her eyes, "I'm frightened too. If Hannah was killed then they want to kill all of us."

"Stop blubbering like an idiot, you idiot. Who is this 'they' who you think wants to kill all of you?"

"The people up there. The people who give orders." She was pointing at the ceiling.

"You're a fool, Agathe. *I* am the people up there, the people who give orders. Do you think I want to kill you?"

Now she cowered. "I hope not. Oh please, can't I go home?"

"Shame on you, Agathe, shame on you. When you were being trained, they told me you had a great potential. Now look at you. Weeping, wringing your hands, afraid of your own shadow. You disgust me." He left her cowering in the hallway, and wondering where indeed Kriegman had disappeared to.

As Agathe hurried to her room, she thought back to her conversation with Kriegman in the library, which was always a safe haven for them to meet in when the others were at the studio.

Kriegman had said, "One of them murdered Hannah. It had to

be. I'm positive. And if they considered her a threat to them, then all of us who posed as Wolheims are in danger."

"But I think she was murdered because she wanted to go home, and they didn't want her back there."

"Don't you want to go home? *I* want to go home. I hate this rotten place with its palm trees and tennis courts. And look at me. He makes me play the butler. 'Kriegman do this, Kriegman do that, Kriegman kiss my backside.' Me! A graduate of Hamburg University with a degree in philosophy. And I let them draft me into espionage. What a fool I am, what a fool. Well let me tell you this, Agathe, I'm not going to wait around waiting for the axe to fall. One of *them* killed Hannah. Maybe Guiss himself."

Her eyes widened. "You think?"

"It's possible," he insisted. "The man is a cold-hearted brute. He has no ethics, he has no morals, he's a party machine. Who is he anyway? Where does he come from? I think he was invented."

"What?" She was incredulous.

"He's not real. The man is not real. There is something about him that does not ring true. I always feel he is acting a role. And some day he'll be unmasked. If I could only find out who it is that *he* answers to."

"You mean he's not the big cheese?"

"He's a big cheese, all right, but of a very inferior brand. Be cautious, Agathe. Be careful. We are in danger. You, me, the boys. We are in terrible danger."

Now she was in her room, but she couldn't lock the door. She jammed a chair under the doorknob and sat on the bed, palms wet again, hands in her lap and trembling, and wondering what to do. Try and run away, but where would she go? Turn herself in to the authorities and plead for mercy? They would put her in jail, but so what? Jail is preferable to death. She had seen those American pictures about women's jails. It wouldn't be so bad, not if kindly Jane Darwell was the warden.

"What are you doing here so late?"

Von Stroheim startled Lisa and Gruber. He had entered the set quietly and Lisa was surprised to see Alysia Hoffman was with him. They found Gruber in the act of photographing the Dauphin's throne. Lisa was a good actress. "You're still here?"

"Obviously. I was just taking Alysia to dinner. What are you doing, Gruber?"

"I'm taking snapshots of the set for Miss Garbo." Quick thinking, thought Lisa.

"And what does she want with snapshots of the set?"

Lisa answered for Gruber. "For her scrapbooks. She keeps insisting this film is her swan song and she wants snapshots for the future to jog her memory of the good time she's having now."

"She's enjoying doing this film?"

"Hell yes," said Lisa, "it's got her in a marvelous frame of mind. Can't you see it in the rushes?"

Alysia finally spoke. "Yes, it's very evident. She even looks younger. Come on, Von, you see it, admit it."

Von, thought Lisa. The lady moves fast. She wants to be a star again. Good luck to you, dearie.

Von Stroheim laughed. "Yes, she's magical. All right, take your pictures and I'll see you in the morning. Wait a minute. I'd like to have a look at that camera." Gruber handed it to him. Von Stroheim held it up so that Alysia Hoffman could have a closer look at it. "I've never seen anything like it before. It's certainly not an American make, is it?"

Lisa said, "I think Greta said it came from South America. Some friend or some fan sent it to her."

"It has to be foreign," agreed Von Stroheim, "it's much too sophisticated to be one of our brands." He handed the camera back to Gruber. "Lisa, remind me to ask Greta where she got it. I'd like to get one for my son. Come Alysia. How's about Romanoff's? I feel in a festive mood tonight. Maybe Bogie will be there. I enjoy trading insults with him."

Lisa watched them leave as Gruber stood, seemingly immobilized. Lisa said, "Our Alysia is a smooth worker."

Gruber answered, "Very smooth. We have enough pictures. Let's get out of here."

"Greta has to be primed about the camera and the snapshots.

Let's go to the office and phone her, then we can drop the film off at Schwab's drugstore. Maybe some movie producer is there waiting to discover me like Lana Turner."

Guiss sat in his study, staring into the fireplace at the pyre of crackling wood which reminded him of Jeanne d'Arc's fate. Between the palms of his hands he warmed a brandy snifter. He was preoccupied with the sudden defection of his comrades and annoyed at having been abandoned without warning. True, they frequently went about their private business without advising him of their plans, but the past month they had been almost inseparable and now he was feeling a mortal emotion, loneliness, and he didn't like being alone. How does Garbo manage it? She relishes it, she treasures it, she husbands her loneliness like a miser, like the miser ZaSu Pitts so brilliantly limned in von Stroheim's *Greed.* He sipped the brandy and was so preoccupied with his thoughts that he did not hear Henkel enter.

"Drinking alone?" Guiss was startled and made a noise that sounded like a puppy's yelp. "That's very bad."

"You startled me." Then sternly, "Where did you disappear to?"

"I felt like some gefilte fish, so I drove to Cantor's on Fairfax Avenue."

"I won't put that in my daily report."

Henkel was lighting a cigar. "Who cares. You admit, there are a few things the Jews have given the world that are a worthwhile legacy. Gefilte fish, knishes, stuffed derma, bagels and lox. I think I'll join you in a brandy."

"Kriegman has defected," said Guiss.

"Oh? Are you sure?"

"I missed him at dinner, which I ate alone." Henkel didn't look guilty. "I went to his room. It was in complete disarray as though he had packed hastily. I looked for his passport but it was also gone. He has fled, the fool. And Agathe is frightened too. I had a talk with her. I hope she isn't thinking of doing anything foolish."

"Why don't we make sure she doesn't?"

"Gustav, would you want it to appear that the Hamburg monster has relocated to Hollywood?"

Henkel shrugged as he crossed to a seat near Guiss while taking a sip of his brandy. "There's only been one murder, Hannah's. That hardly constitutes an epidemic. Did her murder cause you to take any flak?"

"Strangely enough, no."

"Well then. . . ."

"I wonder where Werner has gone. He rarely goes off by himself," said Guiss.

"Perhaps he felt an urge to patronize Madam Frances tonight." Madam Frances ran movieland's favorite house of prostitution.

"I wouldn't mind a visit myself. Risa has been rather cold to me lately." Guiss sounded petulant.

"Well, you're so obvious about Greta, can you blame her?"

"Nothing will come of a relationship with Greta. I think the woman's asexual."

"That's not what I've heard. I hear she possesses quite a scrapbook of sexual memories." He contemplated his cigar and then said. "We have never discussed the detectives, Albert."

"Villon and Lake? They're a music hall act."

"I have taken the liberty to investigate Villon and Lake."

Guiss was surprised and pleased. "So? What have you found? Anything incriminating?"

Henkel spoke slowly and deliberately. "Villon is a highly respected police officer. On some cases I find he was as ruthless in tracking down a killer as Javert was in his pursuit of Valjean." He took a puff of cigar.

"And Mr. Lake?"

"He is not a member of the Los Angeles Police Department."

"Perhaps he's a reporter."

"Reporters can't afford to live in the Garden of Allah. I think he's a federal agent."

Guiss's face hardened. "If he is, he's no match for me."

"Still, if he is, then it means we are in danger."

"Why so? We're producing a film. Lots of aliens have set up

independent production here. So it stands to reason we have too."

"But if they investigate where our funds are coming from?"

"Yes, there's a danger there. But still, that's part of our job, no? Danger is always with professionals like us. Come Gustav, I'm still hungry. Let's go raid the refrigerator."

"You think?"

"I positively think," said Arnold.

They were in Villon's office. After leaving Garbo, they'd decided to do some work and picked up sandwiches and coffee for their dinner. Now it was three hours later and they had put on paper everything they knew about the *Joan the Magnificent* production. They listed the cast of characters involved: not just the actors, but also those who were participating behind the scenes. Arnold was waiting to hear from Washington as to the true identities of the Wolheim family. Surely one of their operatives in Europe, and there were a brilliant assortment risking their lives in Germany, would soon provide them with that information.

Now Arnold had posited the theory that Guiss wasn't the head of this operation. He had a hunch Guiss was taking his orders from someone superior. "And that someone had Mrs. Wolheim murdered. And murder can be infectious. It can spread. I think we're in for a few more killings."

"How tiresome, dahling," said Villon archly and then stretched his arms. "What about von Stroheim and Alysia Hoffman?" Lisa Schmidt had phoned them and told them of hers and Gruber's encounter with the director and the actress, after which she phoned Garbo and advised her to back up the lie that she had requested photos of the set and that the camera was her property.

"Von Stroheim, who knows? Alysia, an unknown quantity. Obviously she's on the make with von Stroheim. She was once a big star, she wants to be a big star again. She ain't the kid she was twenty years ago, but then, in the movie business, who can make a safe guess?"

"I must admit," began Villon, "I was quite impressed by her having worked all over Europe. I suppose in the silent days it didn't matter. She must have piled up a big list of contacts."

"Indeed. It got her to Mexico and then into the States."

"Do you suppose she might have known Guiss or any of his bunch back there in Germany?"

Lake rubbed his nose. "We could ask her. But I'm sure she'll say she didn't. Lisa says she's not at all chummy with them at the studio. In fact, the only one she relates to is Greta."

(My Greta, thought Villon, with a silly grin.)

"There's that dumb look on your face again."

"Hmmm? What? Oh, sorry. You were saying?"

"I said the only one she relates to is Greta, who got her the job." He wondered if Herb was suffering a touch of indigestion. "Now she's working on relating to von Stroheim. Well, he spent a lot of time abroad before the war began."

"He made some good pictures in France," said Villon. *"Grand Illusion* is a knockout. And very anti-war. The Nazis didn't make anti-war propaganda films."

"They only made a lot of anti-semitic crap and infantile operettas with Zarah Leander. She's a Swede but she works exclusively for the Nazis. Real weird, them Europeans." Arnold scratched the back of his hand. "Could von Stroheim be a part of this gang? Nobody would touch him for years. Not since 1933 when he was kicked off *Walking Down Broadway* by Fox. After that it was hard times for him. Quickies on Poverty Row. Then all of a sudden he turns up in France and he's a star above the title again."

Villon nodded. "They're much more faithful to the old timers over there. Here we throw them on the ash heap and make believe they never existed. Why is it in this country that aging is an embarrassment?" He picked a crumb from his desk and licked it off his finger. "I don't think von Stroheim's tainted. He just got lucky all of a sudden, and I hope he's prepared to see this whole damn thing blow up in his face. Arnold?"

"What?"

"Couldn't you get Greta a special G-man's badge?"

"Come on, Herb. Grow up!"

"Okay, now as to Alysia Hoffman. . . ."

The lady in question was reading her director's palm. The lighting at Mike Romanoff's restaurant in Beverly Hills was subdued and flattering and there was no Humphrey Bogart for von Stroheim to trade barbs with. In fact the restaurant was suffering a paucity of celebrities, which it usually did on a midweek night. Working actors were at home learning their lines or grabbing some much needed sleep; non-working actors couldn't afford to eat out, let alone at Mike Romanoff's, Mike being a fraud from Brooklyn who claimed to be a scion of Russian royalty. Hollywood was amused by him and the restaurant's food was good.

"What else do you see?" asked von Stroheim, as he signaled the waiter for more champagne. He did not believe in palmistry or astrology or black magic or in an afterlife, but he decided it was politic to humor the woman, who was obviously eager to resume her former station in films as a star.

"I see a very confusing future."

"With a war on, that's inevitable." He moved his hand from hers to his champagne glass. "Tell me, Alysia, when it ends, will you stay here or go back to Germany?"

"Will the war ever end? And Germany. Germany will be in ruins. It will take the film industry a long time to renew itself. By then I'll be forgotten."

"Here they hardly got to know you, your films were rarely exported. But there, you're still a big star."

"You think so? You remember Lil Dagover and Dorothea Wieck?" He did. "Well, they were brought here in the thirties with big hoopla and big fanfare. They were brought as threats to Greta and Marlene. A big laugh. They failed miserably, so back they went to Germany. And back to what? Character roles, small supporting parts, and early retirement."

"Your face changes when you're bitter."

She smiled lavishly. "Is this an improvement?"

"A vast one. Alysia, did you know Guiss or any of the others back in the homeland?"

"Not at all, why do you ask? You sound like the detectives."

"Guiss disturbs me. There's something not right with him."

"How so?"

"I find him terribly unreal. I feel he's an actor who reads his lines well but with no emotion. It's as though someone out of sight is directing his every move, his every intonation."

"You make him sound like he's a robot."

"That's what I think he is. A robot. Now then, my dear, this has been terribly charming, but it's getting late and we have to be on the set bright and early. So, your place or mine?"

"But Miss Garbo, you mustn't go out walking by yourself. It's not safe."

Garbo waved away Lottie's apprehension. "I can look after myself. I have to think. I can't think in the house. The walls are closing in on me. The private guards are all over the beach since the murder. I'll be all right."

"At least carry a blunt instrument! Take this butcher knife."

Garbo laughed. "I wouldn't know how to use it. I'd cut myself and wouldn't that be foolish?"

A few minutes later she was trudging along the beach. She heard an argument between Hearst and Marion Davies as she passed their house, Hearst tweeting away like a cornered canary, Marion shouting epithets that made Garbo cringe. Then a man emerged from out of nowhere, out of the night's blackness and she stood still waiting for him to identify himself. He said nothing, so she spoke. "Who are you? What do you want?"

"Oh it's you, Miss Garbo." Tom Toth recognized that familiar husky voice. "It's me. Tom Toth."

"Oh good, Thomas. You're on the job. You're protecting us."

"I wouldn't wander too far, Miss Garbo. It's a very cloudy night."

"I see that. I just need a little walk. I'll be all right." She continued on her way. He decided to follow her at a safe distance. Soon he was wondering, What's so fascinating to her about the murder house?

What fascinated Garbo was that the front door was slightly ajar. And she could see the faint reflection of dim light, not enough to spill out into the blackout and cause an alarm. It wasn't a matter of overcoming fear or a display of false bravery, it was just her incurable curiosity. She widened the door enough for her slender body to enter the room.

Now why the hell is she going in there, wondered Toth. The murderer returning to the scene of the crime? Murderer? Garbo? Crazy.

Garbo was appalled by the ugliness of the furnishings. There was just enough light for her to regard the room with a look of distaste. The light was coming from the room beyond. She heard no movement there. She was unaware that Toth was at the front door watching her. He saw her push open the door to the next room. It was the kitchen.

Garbo sniffed. Someone had cooked something here. She saw an opened can on the kitchen sink. She crossed the room to investigate. It was a popular brand of corned beef hash, cheap but tasty. She had Lottie prepare it for her every so often. The light came from a small lamp above the stove. It was shaded. Terrible room. Who had come here to eat corned beef hash? she wondered.

And then she knew.

He was seated in the breakfast nook, a terrible look of agony on his face. On the table in front of him were the remnants of what she suspected had been corned beef hash. He still clutched a fork in his right hand. His left was clasped in a fist. He looked like a judge presiding over a courtroom, but the condemned was himself.

Behind her, Tom Toth said, "Jesus Christ."

"No," Garbo corrected him calmly, "this is Kriegman, who has also been Mr. Wolheim. I hope the phone is still working. We have to phone for help."

Seventeen

By God they found another stiff in that joint!" Marion Davies shouted from her balcony. "Greta found it, for crying out loud. Greta of all people! Silent Sam who wants to be alone. Don't that take the cake!" She took a swig from her glass of borscht, which held a healthy jigger of tequila. Hearst came charging onto the balcony.

Hearst tweeted, "She's not talking to any reporters. She's barricaded in her house with those two harpies of hers, Viertel and de Acosta. Go over there, Marion. See if she'll talk to you. She trusts you."

"Oh God. That means I have to get dressed. I can't tramp over there in these pajamas." She shouted for her maid. "Get me that blue pailleted special out of the closet, my pink picture hat with the yellow ribbons and my pink slippers with the sapphire buckles. No you can't have this glass, I'm not finished with it!"

Hearst now sounded like a piccolo. He asked sternly, "What's in that glass?"

"Borscht!" she yelled. "The Reds are our allies now, right? They drink Borscht. Now I drink borscht. It's all for the Allied cause." She took a healthy swig, smacked her lips, and blessed Hearst for buying all her lies. Now that's true love.

Kriegman's murder cornered the airwaves. It was broadcast across the country and around the world by short wave. The Santa Monica Poison Case had taken on significant importance now that there was a second victim. There were those who considered that, wherever Kriegman's soul had landed, he should be flattered his body was discovered by the great Garbo. Kriegman caused no tug of war between Villon and the Santa Monica police force. It was tacitly agreed to leave the case in the very capable hands of Villon and Arnold Lake. Actually, Santa Monica's force was a small one, and they couldn't successfully tackle a murder case.

The scene of the crime was of necessity, because of the late hour, basking in the glow of an arc light, breaching the blackout policy. The authorities doubted there would be any Japanese planes in the area. They were capable of making it to Hawaii, but getting to the California coast was considered an impossibility. Villon's team were all over the place. The coroner was grumbling something about why can't bodies be discovered at a reasonable hour. He also told Villon and Arnold he wouldn't be a bit surprised if this was another case of thallium nitrate poisoning.

This murder gave Villon and Arnold a fix on the killer's modus operandi. Villon said, "It has to have worked this way. Mr. X, that's our killer . . ."

"Why not Madam X too as a possibility?"

Villon agreed, "Definitely a possibility. But for clarity's sake, since clarity begins at home," Arnold grimaced, "let's stay with Mr. X. So he is known and trusted by both victims. He offers them safety until they can disappear out of L.A. and into the hinterlands, the boondocks, South America, wherever they think they'll be safe. Safe not from us, but from their own people. Mr. X, of course, is a fake. His assurances are lies. He has orders to murder the defectors. He knows poisons. He sends Mrs. Wolheim . . . what did you say they told you her real name was?"

"Hannah Baum."

"Let's stick with Wolheim. It simplifies matters. Where was I?"

"He sends Mrs. Wolheim . . ."

"Yes. Right. He sends her to that big undercover operation in the sky gradually; there's no rush at first. But when she begins to become a big pain and an even more dangerous threat, he gets her packing, deposits her luggage at Union Station where we found it and brings her here, presumably to hide until it's time to catch the train. Probably frightens her into thinking the town is crawling with Nazi operatives on the hunt for her. She dies. He leaves her here. Why not? It's as good a place as any and there are no traces left behind that might incriminate him."

"He was obviously in a big rush with Kriegman." Arnold watched the coroner's assistants trying to pry the fork out of Kriegman's hand.

"Obviously. The spokesman at the castle . . . which one was it?"

"Gustav Henkel, the scriptwriter."

"Sure he is. Anyway, he says Kriegman was last seen by one of the maids around three in the afternoon. There's clothes and a suitcase missing from his room, so he must have decided to take it on the lam on the spur of the moment."

Arnold screws up his face, heavy in thought. "How about this? Try this scenario. When Martin Gruber took those candids of him in the garden, he was in a state of agitation, Kriegman. Worried. Frightened. Mrs. Wolheim's death triggered the fear he might be the next target."

Villon spread his hands and said, "And he was right, right?"

"The killer recognized the danger signal. He worked on Kriegman and won his trust. The same routine as with the lady victim. But he had to work fast. He convinced Kriegman he could provide him with a safe exit, but he had to hide out here until it was time to go. Then when they're here, he's conveniently brought along the corned beef hash, offers to fix some for Kriegman, who undoubtedly hasn't had his dinner, and the killer puts enough poison in the food to kill a football team."

"You know that for sure?"

"It has to be. It had to work fast."

The coroner was telling his men as he stood with one hand on Kriegman's shoulder, "Okay, boys. Wrap him and file him."

Villon asked the coroner what he thought killed Kriegman. Could it be thallium nitrate again?

"Absolutely," said the coroner. "A poisoner always stays with the same brand. I assume they feel comfortable with it, it's like the company of an old friend. Oh yes, it was a very heavy dose. Look at his face, if you can stand it. I assume he was wolfing the food down, so before it took effect, he'd finished most of it. Then whammo, it got him and you can see the pain must have been ferocious. Look at the way his legs are splayed under the table. Boy what he must have suffered in his feet." His men were having difficulty removing Kriegman from the breakfast nook. Rigor had set in remarkably fast. "Gently boys, let's try not to bust any bones."

Villon led Arnold out of the kitchen. "What do you think, Arnold? Who's next?"

"Logically, the boys who impersonated the sons and the girl who impersonated the daughter."

"I'm going to assign Greta some protection. Now that she discovered the body, somebody may think she knows more than she really does know, and set her up for a farewell tour. Anyway, there's nothing else we can do around here. I'm sure the killer left no trace. The boys are taking the hash can back to the lab to test for prints, but I doubt they'll find any. Let's drive over to Greta's. I'd walk, but I can't stand sand in my shoes."

Arriving at Garbo's house, they faced a barrage of questions from a small army of reporters and photographers encamped outside. They gave them very little satisfaction, Villon promising them a big break later in the day. Inside the house they found Garbo with Salka and Mercedes. To their pleasant surprise, Marion Davies was there looking like a Christmas tree ablaze out of season. She was drinking from a glass of hot chocolate laced with slivovitz from a flask in her handbag. Greta introduced her to the men and then Greta suggested that Tom Toth, who was guarding the rear of her house with several of his men, escort Davies back to her house. What Garbo had to say to her friends was for their ears only. If Davies heard there was the danger she'd pass it on to Hearst.

"The bum's rush, eh?" said Davies, as Toth offered her his arm. She wasn't too steady on her feet. "It's okay, Greta. I understand. Thanks for the interview. I did interview you, didn't I? That's what Willie sent me to do. Did I get any information? What year is this? Where am I?" She admonished Toth. "Not so fast, Buster, I'm not wasting any of this. Slivovitz is hard to come by these days. Them Poles ain't exporting it anymore, under the circumstances." She downed the remnants of her drink in one gulp and handed the empty glass to Lottie. Then she took Toth's arm and with her free hand waved at the others and said, "See you in church." Toth managed to guide her out to the patio. Lottie shut the door behind them and wondered when Miss Garbo would get any sleep.

"Lottie, you'd better go to bed. I won't be needing you anymore tonight."

"What about yourself? You've got an early call."

"I'll be fine. Please go. There is much for us to discuss here."

"Yes ma'am." This was said peevishly. Lottie was very annoyed at being excluded. She wanted to offer to brew fresh hot chocolate, but since poison was the killer's method, she decided it was wiser not to remind them she too had had a go at it once upon a time.

After Lottie left, Arnold told the ladies Kriegman had been killed in a similar manner as Mrs. Wolheim. Arnold told them Mrs. Wolheim's real name was Hannah Baum. Villon retrieved the narrative and explained how he and Arnold thought the murders had been committed. They were convinced the murderer was in residence at the castle.

Greta accepted a light from Villon and paced about the room, puffing on her cigarette. She was troubled and she saw no reason to disguise her feelings. She recognized there was a possibility that she herself was in danger but sloughed the danger off with a shrug of her shoulders.

Garbo the fearless, thought Villon, wishing desperately to overpower her with passionate kisses. Then he thought of his beloved Hazel Dickson, somewhere in the war zone with her unit, and him left behind because of a punctured eardrum.

Arnold was wishing Villon would wipe that idiotic look off his face.

"I have spent a lot of time with Guiss," said Garbo, now positioned in the center of the room under a grey cloud of cigarette smoke. "I have studied him very carefully and I positively feel there is something wrong with the picture he presents of himself."

"The man is dangerous, Greta," said Mercedes. "Stop playing detective. These men are perfectly capable of solving the murders, I'm sure." Villon refrained from blowing her a kiss.

Garbo said, "My dear, there is more to this situation than the murder of two enemy agents. We must also consider, and most importantly, what further damage the survivors can do to our country. Isn't it possible there are others who pose a threat and must be eliminated? Isn't it possible their subversive activities will continue to spread unchecked like a frightening epidemic? And most importantly of all, certainly very important to me," she said, now directly addressing Villon and Arnold, "What is the truth behind this production? Why are they doing it and for such an absurd sum of money? What's really going on behind the scenes?"

Arnold spoke up. "Greta, as of a couple of hours ago, my office knows a great deal more. We know the real identities of the Wolheims." He told them. "We know the purpose of the production. Certainly the entire five million isn't being spent on the film."

Salka laughed. "Oh no? Wait till von Stroheim gets through with it." Mercedes nodded agreement knowingly.

Said Arnold, "He's begun to economize. My informants tell me he's tightening his belt."

"Yes," agreed Garbo, "he's shooting less unnecessary footage. I think he's averaging three to four minutes of film a day. That's very good for a production like this where there are battle scenes and panoramic episodes that require scores of extras. So Arnold, where is most of the money supposed to go?"

"To continue financing their various organizations in this country. It's as simple and as obvious as that. They have to channel funds here to feed their espionage ring."

"But how did they get these millions into the country this time?" It wasn't a question from Garbo, it was a demand.

"The Germans get the money to Northern Ireland. The Irish have set up dummy corporations in America who receive the money and disburse it."

"But that's terrible!" said Salka.

"Look, Salka," said Arnold. "Northern Ireland has been fighting in vain for their independence for almost three decades. They hate the British. They'll go to any lengths to see them defeated. With Britain overthrown, independence is theirs."

"What are these dummy corporations?" asked Mercedes.

"Sorry," said Arnold, "that's positively privileged information. But just wait until the war is over. The world, and especially Wall Street, will be in for a big shock when we start unmasking the villains."

"So Arnold, here we sit in the eye of a hurricane." Garbo was nibbling absentmindedly at a Hydrox cookie. She looked at her girlfriends and giggled.

"What's so funny?" asked Mercedes.

"Here we are, the three witches of Shakespeare." She intoned spookily, " 'Double double toil and trouble, Cauldron boil, cauldron bubble.' I wanted to play the wicked witch in *The Wizard of Oz* but poor Louis B. had a fit when I asked him. I would have done it for nothing." She sighed a very heavy sigh. "How often am I plagued by minor defeats." Then she tossed the cookie aside onto a table and said to Villon and Arnold, "Boys, let's get back to Albert Guiss. Something about him preys on my mind. He's larger than life. Much much much larger than life. The way he lives, his exaggerated eccentricities. The castle. The dozens in service there, most of them unnecessary. Like who nowadays hires a majordomo to oversee the kitchen? Utterly ridiculous. And those spear holders in their silly uniforms." She laughed. "It's all so dumb. But when the magazines ask to photograph the interiors, they are met with an iron curtain of silence. No publicity, thank you very much. This pompous and ridiculous display is for our own pleasure. Tell me if I'm wrong, chaps, but don't you get the suspicion that Guiss is not his own master?"

"Smart lady," said Arnold, expecting Garbo to preen with pride, but she was too anxious to get on with other matters bothering her.

"Don't misread me, I'm sure that in many ways Albert Guiss is a very powerful man, but tell me, Arnold. Your people were so magnificent in uncovering the identities of the Wolheims and so many other facts of importance, why don't they know the source of Guiss's wealth? Or do they?"

"We don't know for sure. We strongly suspect he's a front for a powerful group of financiers."

"Well then, who are these financiers?" Garbo looked at the women, anxious for them to share her curiosity.

"We don't know," Arnold replied truthfully. "We can take pot-shots and guess, but we don't know for sure."

Garbo asked provocatively, almost flirting, "So what do you guess?"

Arnold played the game. "You're a smart lady. What do you think we guess?"

"Ha ha ha. All right, I'll tell you. I think Albert Guiss was created to be an investor in the overthrow of the free world. I think over the past decade or whatever it took, the members of the Axis made Albert Guiss into this overblown financial creature who could travel the world freely and without suspicion, making the necessary investments they needed to build the powerful war machine intended to destroy the Allies. Do I make sense?"

"Greta, have you had access to our files?" Arnold was impressed.

"You know I haven't. I'm just having a wonderful time discovering sections of my brain I've never had any reason to use before. Salka, Mercedes, let me be an example to both of you. Worry less about scripts and refugees and concentrate more on activating your minds into fresh areas of discovery."

"Smugness doesn't become you," said Salka. "It's late, I think it's time we all went home and let Greta get some sleep. Gentlemen, I'm sure you realize Greta herself might be in danger. Since she's so quick to share her delightful deductions with everyone, it's bound to occur to Guiss and his odious satellites that she might just deduce herself into a proper solution. Oh God, Greta, must you be so suicidal?"

"How can I help myself? I'm a Swede. We have the highest percentage of suicide in the whole world. Can you imagine that? It must be all those months of winter darkness. Goodnight, my darlings. Get home safely. No Arnold, you and Herbert wait a few moments. I'm not finished with you."

Villon thought of offering to spend the night, but what would happen if he ever was invited to share her bed, he wondered, and immediately supplied the answer. He'd be a nervous, fumbling wreck and she and her friends would have a big laugh over it.

Now the three were alone. "I had to get rid of them," said Greta, "they fuss and fret over me as though I was something fragile. I'm not. I'm a pretty strong fellow. Feel my muscle, go ahead, feel it." It was a very strong muscle. Villon wondered if she'd be interested in some Indian hand wrestling.

Feeling re-energized now that they had humored her, Garbo resumed a serious demeanor. "Now then, men, there is a murderer out there who is a threat to our friends. Lisa and Gruber are certainly in danger, aren't they?" Arnold nodded. "Do you know something, I have this intuitive feeling Guiss is very angry about these murders. I am sure to him they were unnecessary."

"What makes you think that?" asked Villon.

"Murder attracts the wrong kind of attention, doesn't it? Like here Kriegman is murdered and Kriegman was Albert's butler and I'm sure this brings the police and the press to his doorstep and it is certainly attention he does not want. Right, men?"

"Absolutely right," said Arnold.

"So Guiss is not the murderer. It could be Werner Lieb, or Gustav Henkel, possibly Risa Barron. . . ." She thought for a moment. "What do they say about poison? Poison is a woman's weapon, yes?"

"Yes," said Villon, "poison can be catnip to a woman. There's been a lot of them dosing their victims."

"And Risa Barron is so charming, I truly find her charming. I envy her that ability. I have to work so hard at it."

Faker, thought Villon.

"Risa is the kind that could lull a person into a false sense of security. She could convince a frightened person that she will help them to safety, she has that way with her. Sad, under other circumstances, she and I might have become friends. I am always attracted to strong women, strong people. Salka and Mercedes are very strong. Take Salka, as an example. Her house is where all the brilliant minds in exile converge. Some day I will take you to one of her salons. There you'll see Einstein and other great scientists. The world's greatest authors. Thomas Mann, Lion Feuchtwanger, Ferenc Molnár. The conversation is dazzling, overwhelming, and I, I the supposed great Garbo, I shrink into a corner and pray they will not notice me."

"After your display of knowledge tonight," said Arnold, "I think if you want to, you could hold your own with them."

"Don't let me kid you, I do hold my own. After all, I'm Garbo. They aren't. But Garbo is a façade created by Hollywood. Behind that façade, as I'm sure you have guessed, hides a very frightened little girl. But enough of this." She paused to light a new cigarette. "Arnold, Herbert, I'm going to say something that you're going to think, quite possibly, is very silly. It's very melodramatic, something that belongs in a film starring Basil Rathbone."

"Let's hear it," said Arnold.

"I think the person who gives Albert Guiss his instructions is here, here in Los Angeles. I really believe such a person exists, and we probably have met this person. This person is much more powerful than Guiss, and therefore much more dangerous. What do you think? Is it logical or is it foolish melodrama?"

Arnold Lake said, "I think you're right on the nose again, Greta."

She clapped her hands. "Well then, I think it's up to me to find and unmask this mysterious creature." Her eyes narrowed. "And I'm pretty sure I can do it. Don't try to discourage me. It's an incentive to do something for my country. Oh yes, it's my country. I shall become a citizen." She smiled sweetly, "And when I do, I hope you'll be there as my witnesses." She clapped her hands again. "And then we'll go to some quiet saloon near the courthouse and get pleasantly drunk and maybe reveal secrets about ourselves to each other that are better left . . . ah well. What are secrets really? They are so unimportant. Do I sound foolish?"

Villon spoke from his heart. "You sound wonderful. And I love you."

"Of course," said Garbo, "of course."

Eighteen

In less than a week, the unsolved murders were consigned to near limbo by the press. The war reclaimed the headlines. The *Joan the Magnificent* company was working at full speed. Von Stroheim astonished everyone, especially Guiss, with his accelerated energies. It was almost at a point where the set builders couldn't keep up with him. He shouted less and was politer when he demanded something. He wasn't subtle about his feelings for Alysia Hoffman, and no one was too surprised when he elevated her to the featured role of one of the Dauphin's courtesans. No longer was she in danger of being beheaded as one of Joan's fellow prisoners. There was doubt, anyway, in the research department, that any form of guillotine existed as yet; otherwise, why not lop Joan's head off instead of burning her at the stake?

Garbo was pleased for Alysia and told her so. "Are you in love with Von?"

Alysia didn't commit herself. "He's been nice to me. He's separated from his wife. He adores his son. He doesn't seem to have many friends and I have a very good time with him. Is this wrong?"

"Of course not," Garbo reassured her, "as long as you recognize that Von is not a man given to permanent commitments. He had a number of mistresses when he worked in France and believe me, I'm not being catty if I warn you there might be some competition of yours in the vicinity."

Alysia laughed. "That doesn't bother me. I live only for the day."

"How wise. Just as I do."

Martin Gruber materialized. He was carrying a large florist's box. Lottie Lynton sniffed and said, "More flowers."

"From Mr. Guiss of course," said Gruber with a small smile.

Garbo said to Alysia, "He inundates me with flowers. I send them to local hospitals. What has come over him?"

"Oh you're very funny, Greta. This past week you've gone off with him after the day's shooting at least three times that I know of."

Garbo assumed a haughty air. "You mustn't count, Alysia. It's bad luck." She said to Gruber, "The snapshots were excellent, Martin. You're a very good photographer."

Alysia said, "Didn't Von want to know where he could buy one of those cameras?"

"That's right, Martin asked me. But I'm totally in the dark. I haven't the vaguest idea if they're available in this country."

Gruber said, "I've made some inquiries. I canvassed some camera shops. They offer no hope. It seems to be of a kind not available here."

Alysia said, "Maybe it's one of a kind."

Garbo was at the dressing table, lightening her eye shadow. "Wouldn't that be unusual? Surely it is unprofitable just to manufacture one camera, one teeny teeny camera. Imagine if General Electric manufactured only one refrigerator, or one toaster. Ha! There would be economic chaos. You know, I was thinking of offering the camera to Erich as a gift when the picture finishes, but now I can't find it. Lottie and I hunted high and low for it, but we can't find it."

Lottie said from the kitchenette, "Well I don't recall ever seeing the damn thing in the house. Are you sure Mr. Gruber gave it back to you?"

"I'm very sure," said Garbo.

"I remember returning it," said Gruber. "Lisa was there when I gave it to you."

"Don't worry about it, Martin. It doesn't matter. I have plenty of other cameras and this one will turn up again. I'm always misplacing things and then find them days later. Martin, tell Mr. Guiss I will thank him in person for the flowers. Later."

Martin left and Alysia watched Lottie arranging the long-stemmed roses in a vase. The others didn't notice her arcane expression.

Sam Goldwyn was listening to Sophie Gang's litany of memos.

"Mrs. Goldwyn called and said she's received a cash donation for her children's relief society. It's a large sum but there was no card or anything and she doesn't know who to thank."

"So why should she bother? It's a synonymous donation."

"I gave Mr. Guiss your budget for *Up in Arms,* and he said he'll let you know in a few days if he's interested in investing."

"The hell with him. Who needs his money? You know I always do my own financing. Go get the budget back."

Sophie was aghast. "I can't do that. That would be impolite."

"I don't like that man anyway. There's something wrong with him. He never eats in the dining room with the rest of us pheasants. Who does he think he is? Hitler? The bum."

Sophie cast a "Heaven help us" glance at the ceiling and returned to her notes. "New York called. They're sending us a very interesting set of galleys. A book Random House is publishing next fall. They're very high on it."

"So what's it about?" He bit off the end of a cigar.

"It's about euthanasia."

"Oh for heaven's seven, Sophie. Why would I want to do a picture about Chinese teenagers?"

Werner Lieb was in Guiss's office in the studio with Henkel and Risa Barron. Guiss was exuberant about the picture's progress and said, "Von Stroheim is really doing an extraordinary job. It's a vast improvement on those first awful days."

Risa said, as she fingered her necklace of lapus lazuli, "Alysia Hoffman has had a tonic effect on him. Now she has a bigger role. Greta better look out. Soon Hoffman might be playing Joan. Don't make such a face, Henkel."

"She doesn't have it in her to be Joan. What are those pictures you're looking at, Werner?"

Lieb removed the monocle from his eye, blew breath on it, and then polished it with a handkerchief. "These are pictures of the set taken by Martin with a very strange, very unique camera." He told them about his incident with Martin and the camera earlier that week, in fact the day Kriegman was murdered.

"So these are the photographs he took?" said Guiss. "He gave you this set?"

"Yes he did. He promised I'd have a look, I found the camera so unique. He said he took them at Greta's request."

"That's right," said Guiss. "She showed them to me. They're quite good."

Werner Lieb agreed. "They're excellent." He handed the set to Risa, who wasn't very interested in the pictures and passed them on to Henkel. Lieb continued, "Kriegman was murdered on the fourteenth. The developers always date the film on the back. Turn one over, Henkel. What's the date?"

"The sixteenth."

"Yes. So these are not the snapshots from the film in the camera when I spoke to Martin in the hallway. These films were shot at a later date. So what he had on the film in the camera was obviously something entirely different."

Henkel asked, "You think he used the camera to photograph something else?"

Lieb said, "Am I the only one among us who has noticed that Martin and Lisa appear to be very very friendly?"

"Well, what's wrong with that?" asked Risa. "She's young and pretty and he's young and handsome. How did they used to say in silent pictures, 'Youth calls to youth?'"

Lieb continued. "Peter Lorre thought she was the woman on the beach the night we were spied on."

"So?" questioned Guiss. "He just as quickly said he was mistaken."

"Much too quickly," said Lieb. "Supposing she really was that woman. And they got to Lorre in order to protect her. His eyesight is damned good."

"He's on dope, Werner," said Risa wearily. She was bored with actors. She was bored with film making. She wanted to be in Brazil, in Rio, where most of her friends had decamped to. Where they were living high on the hog. She was bored with international intrigue. She was tired of looking over her shoulder to see if she was being followed. And she was bored with the men in this room and their constant presence.

Lieb spoke calmly, coolly and with authority. "I think Lisa Schmidt was that woman on the beach. I think Martin Gruber was given that sophisticated camera to photograph Kriegman because Greta suspected he was Wolheim. Gruber got his photograph and Garbo made a positive identification and so Kriegman was eliminated."

Guiss leaned on the desk with his elbows and made a pyramid of his fingers. "Why would they eliminate him? Why not arrest him? The sensible thing would be for the federals to take him into custody and interrogate him mercilessly. You know, the way we've seen Edward G. Robinson do it. It makes no sense that they killed Kriegman and Hannah Baum. It makes no sense at all. It's totally illogical."

Risa Barron had a new cigarette holder. It was decorated with tiny chips of valuable gems. She took a puff, a long and languorous one, exhaled, and then said matter-of-factly, "Now Greta is a threat to the others." She was enjoying the look of annoyance on Guiss's face. "She can identify Agathe and the three boys. If Agathe is arrested, I think she'll go over to the other side to save her neck. Kriegman's murder didn't do much to improve her shaky morale." She chuckled. "The smallest sounds make her jump with fear. Do you know, just this morning she likened the clatter of the lawn mower to a machine-gun attack. Can you imagine that? And Albert, why do we need so many gardeners? They're all over the place. It's impossible to stroll the grounds without one of them popping out from behind a tree or a bush to scare the hell out of me. But I must say the pool crew are so young and attractive. Don't you agree, Albert? Greta is a threat to our security?"

"If she ever was, she no longer is."

"You sound so positive," said Risa.

"I have reason to believe Greta regrets having cooperated with the authorities. You know how she treasures her privacy. Since finding Kriegman's body, her life has been hell. She is besieged by reporters and cameramen at her beach house. You've seen them yourselves at the entrance to the studio, lying in ambush for her. Now she's impatient to complete the film and leave Hollywood."

"To go where?"

They had been strolling the castle grounds a few nights earlier, Garbo with her arms folded, a sweater around her shoulders to fend off the night chill, Guiss with his arm around her shoulder. Of late when he made that move she didn't shrug it away. It was obvious to her he was in love with her. She recognized the signs. She was still a master at the art of creating lovers. She said huskily, "There is an unhealthy atmosphere here in Hollywood. It's not just the war, it's the industry itself. The Jews have a stranglehold on the industry. Mayer, the Warner brothers, Sam Goldwyn. Now there's this influx of Jews from Europe and they too have become infected with this need, this sick desire for power. I don't like it. I have to get away."

"Where will you go?"

"I'm giving that some thought. For a while I'm thinking of relocating to New York City. There I'll wait for the war to end. Then I will go to Switzerland. Salka has a house there in Gstaad."

"And Salka is one Jew who does not seek power?" He had removed his hand from her shoulder and was lighting a cigarette.

"Have you never known a Jew you liked?"

"I've never had much traffic with them."

"You're pulling my leg!"

"I wish I was."

"Be serious. You haven't dealt with Jewish financiers? How could you avoid that, you silly man."

Guiss's face froze. "I am not a silly man. Those who I deal with in finances mean nothing to me. I don't care what their origins are, only the financial condition of their empires. I learned long ago to be emotional about nothing. I'm a tough trader, Greta, and that's because socially I keep those in power at arm's length. Yes, I have a drink with them, of necessity I dine with them, there have been occasions when I took trips with them, but I have a strict rule: never become intimate with them."

She laughed. "You're so contradictory. Here I am, alone with you under the stars, in a garden that is heavenly scented, gloriously scented, you have had your arm around me, this is not intimate?"

"This is not a business transaction. This is a man and a woman," he took her hand and kissed it, and then he whispered, "I want to give you the world, Greta."

"I don't want the world," she said impatiently. "It is much too much to manage. And besides, to offer me the world now is to offer me damaged goods. If the world was mine I'd be responsible for repairing and reconstructing all the ruined cities, the ruined nations. What an appalling thought."

"I will make you the queen of the European film industry."

"Ah, now you are diminishing your offer. First you offer me the world, and now you narrow your offer down to Europe." She decided the time was right to take the plunge. "Tell me the truth, Albert. You're a friend of Hitler's, aren't you?" They were standing in the shadow of a gazebo. There was little light from the stars and the crescent moon. She couldn't see his face clearly, but from his intake of breath, she knew she had struck a nerve. "I need to know, Albert. It's important to my future."

"Why?" The manner in which he spoke the word gave her no clue as to his feelings.

"I'll tell you why and you will respect this confidence, as I certainly will respect yours. Before the war, Hitler made me an offer through his embassy here to return to Germany and make films there. He promised me the run of the UFA studios. Magnificent real estate. I hope the Allies don't bomb it into oblivion. I think of some day owning it. I turned the offer down because not only did I then think it was presumptuous, but because my career was on an upturn thanks to the success of *Ninotchka.*"

"You were surrounded by Jews on that one."

"Very gifted ones—Lubitsch, Billy Wilder, Melvyn Douglas."

"Ina Claire?"

"Good God no, she's a *shicksa.* A very wicked woman. Did you know she married my John Gilbert after I stood him up at the altar? Never mind, it's not important. It's ancient history and I am not a historian. What I have been doing of late, Albert, is a lot of thinking about myself and my future as an actress. If there is a future for me, it's no longer in this country. It will have to be in Europe. I speak many languages. My native Swedish, French, my Spanish is not bad, and I'm very fluent in German. If you have a direct line to Hitler, and his offer is still open, then I am interested."

"Bravo! Bravo Greta!" He took her in his arms and kissed her with a fervent passion that took her by surprise. She struggled for air.

"Why Albert, your ardor is such a revelation!"

"I'm insane about you!"

"Oh don't be insane, insanity is so difficult for me to cope with. I always thought my father was insane and he was such a brute."

He continued holding her in his arms, strafing her ears with words she was anxious to repeat to Villon and Arnold. "Bravo, not becuase you are ready to return to the Fatherland, but Bravo because your words fill me with confidence, that you feel sure we will win the war . . ."

Fatherland. We will win the war. And yet why do I not struggle out of his arms? Why? Because I'm a good soldier. I am also a spy, and if I must say so myself, a damned good one.

". . . that we will prevail," continued Guiss without pausing to take a breath, "Greta, Greta, my enchanting Greta, my exquisite jewel, when all this is finished, marry me, oh my darling, marry me."

"When all what is finished? You mean the picture? Surely there will be retakes."

He released her. She patted some stray hairs back into place. "You're jesting," he said. "You're making fun of me."

"The thought of marriage usually disturbs me. I am not a person to be bound by a ring and a piece of paper. If we must, we will talk about it some other time. I'm sorry, Albert. Marriage has never been for me and I don't think it ever will be. So if our relationship is predicated on that, then perhaps we should both forget this conversation, try to make believe it never took place."

He watched her as she strolled away from him. His words brought her to a halt. "I will not forget this conversation. I love you too much. I will contact Goebbels and he will tell Adolf. I'm sure despite severe losses on the battlefields, they will be very pleased. Eva Braun is a great fan of yours." Garbo shuddered. "I'm sure you girls will have a great deal to talk about when you meet."

"If we find something in common," said Garbo. She led him back to the castle.

She was frightened. She had learned too much. Guiss will tell his unholy threesome what they discussed and someone in that group won't buy her desire to return to Germany. But still, she reminded herself, I'm a soldier on a mission and I knew when I accepted it that it would be terribly dangerous. I am no longer frightened. I am proud of myself. Very proud of myself. And Villon and Arnold Lake will be proud of me too. And perhaps if Arnold can't make me a G-woman, he'll make me a Junior G-man. I eat the breakfast cereal that sponsors them and I listen to that radio show religiously, along with "Portia Faces Life" and "Just Plain Bill."

Risa Barron couldn't stop laughing. She had this hilarious vision of Garbo and Eva Braun exchanging dress patterns.

"Control yourself, Risa," said Guiss sternly.

"I can't help it. Eva Braun is such an idiot!" The laughter continued.

Werner Lieb said, "Well, now Miss Greta Garbo might know just a bit too much about us."

Guiss slammed his fist down on the desk. "She's completely trustworthy! I'm sure of that! Last night we became lovers."

Risa paled and jammed a cigarette into the holder. She said coldly, "Congratulations." She wasn't provoked by jealousy. She wasn't given to the common, ordinary emotions of her sisters. To women like Risa Barron, men were a commodity, especially very rich men. There had been others before Guiss and there would be others succeeding him. She'd done very well by him, her treasury of jewels, the investments he made for her. She was extremely well off, and was determined to survive the war and whatever consequences of Germany's defeat. She had arranged a safe exit to South America months before the conflict became a reality. She had something else on her mind and she voiced it. "So now there are three to occupy our attention. Lisa Schmidt, Martin Gruber and Miss Greta Garbo."

"Risa, I'm warning you." The threat in Guiss's voice was unmistakable.

There was a trace of a smile on the woman's face. "Love can be so destructive." Then she raised her voice, "It has paralyzed your brain! You, the great genius created by even greater geniuses, you've become a lovesick schoolboy. It's a cliché but it's true."

"There must be no more murders." Guiss had their undivided attention. "It was foolish to murder Hannah and Kriegman. Absolutely foolish. The police and the federals wouldn't be on our trail now if they had continued to live." No one refuted his statement. "Did you hear me, Werner?"

"I've heard an awful lot," said Lieb, while Gustav Henkel stifled one of his nervous yawns.

"And I will hear nothing further about Greta Garbo. We've seen von Stroheim's assemblage. This film is their masterpiece, and in a way," he added with pride, "it is *my* masterpiece too!" He stood up and proclaimed proudly, "Around the world, millions will read," he said, waving his arm like an orchestra conductor, "Albert Guiss presents Greta Garbo in Erich von Stroheim's *Joan the Magnificent*. If I must say so myself, it sounds most impressive." He sat down, a faraway look in his eyes. It did not bother him that his associates were displeased and angry. He was not aware he was seated on a powder keg. He was wrapped in his selfish thoughts of future glory, of a future to be shared with Greta Garbo, and it did not occur to him that these dreams were the components of his Achilles' heel.

Garbo had a rendezvous with Villon and Arnold at Salka Viertel's house. It was agreed that they would not meet at the studio ever again, unless there was an official reason for a police visit. The beach house would remain out of bounds until the press would abandon their pursuit of the star.

"So now Salka, you are part of the war. Your home is our safe house! Don't you feel proud that you are contributing something?"

Salka sniffed and went to the study and her enemy, the typewriter. She hated working but she needed money to survive. She had to support a variety of friends who were down on their luck. She worked hard so they would never be down on *her* luck. She sat at the typewriter, let herself dwell on Garbo for just a few more seconds, and then erased the word "danger" from her mind and tried to compose some dialogue for Joan Crawford.

Garbo told Villon and Arnold everything. She had a powerful memory and she acted out brilliantly the scene in the garden with Albert Guiss. She heavily underlined "Fatherland" and "We will win the war" and insisted it was now quite evident to her that he was a creation of the Axis allies. She didn't tell them she had slept with Guiss. Something like that called for discretion and she was the master of discreet.

Arnold said, "It's not as though we weren't pretty positive they were German operatives, but at least now we've got it from the horse's mouth."

"What? Garbo? A horse's mouth?" she said with mock indignity. "Salka thinks I'm the other end of the horse! Ha ha ha! So I have done well, yes?"

"Absolutely brilliant," said Arnold.

"So now I can become a Junior G-man?" She had come to the rendezvous with Lottie, directly from the studio, and Lottie had immediately commandeered the kitchen to prepare snacks and her inevitable hot chocolate. While she laid these out on the coffee table in the living room where they were conferring, Arnold marveled at Garbo's contradictions.

She was a great star, a strong woman seemingly in command of herself and her destiny, whatever that might be, and yet there was this charming and amusing childish side of her. Calling them "chaps" and "men" and wanting to be a "G-woman" or even a "Junior G-man". Or was she kidding the pants off them? She wasn't a particularly witty woman, but she had a marvelous sense of humor. Her friends adored her and she seemed to adore them in return. Still, there was something about her he found sad and touching. Her desire to be alone. Her fierce determination to remain her own person. Did she have relatives? he wondered. And if so, would they be there for her should she ever need them?

Villon was saying, "Interesting they selected Goldwyn's studio to do the production. I mean Sam Goldwyn, how Jewish can you get? I don't suppose you've heard Guiss refer to him as 'that yid' or something equally unpleasant?"

"No, not Guiss, he's quite gentlemanly about his dislikes and distastes. But you remind me. It was someone else who referred to Jews as 'yids.' I ignored it then, but now . . . it makes me wonder. Hot chocolate, anyone?"

Nineteen

The bottle of milk was on the floor in the hallway next to the door to Lisa Schmidt's apartment. The milk was delivered early and Lisa enjoyed her varieties of dry cereal and milk for breakfast. Occasionally there wasn't enough time and she'd wait until she got to the studio to eat. This morning there was plenty of time. She brought the bottle of milk to her small dining table and poured it over the krispies. She noticed the bottle cap was slightly awry; it had been like that several other times. She must leave the milkman a note and tell him to stop being so careless. He was a replacement, she learned from a neighbor. The war had claimed his predecessor.

As she ate slowly, she dwelled on many things. The Guiss gang, as she privately referred to them, the picture, and von Stroheim's interest in Alysia Hoffman. Then there was Hoffman herself, a dethroned movie queen desperately in search of a new kingdom. Martin Gruber and the chances he took with the camera, hell, the chances they were all taking, and there was that burning sensation in her feet again. It came and it went, all week long, always in the morning when she ate breakfast at home. Burning sensation in the feet . . . *oh my God.*

She phoned Villon. She was positive she was being poisoned, she told him. Her breakfast milk. No, she wasn't panicking, but she was frightened. She didn't know how much poison was in her system. She wasn't sure how much milk she had drunk, but she got a quart a day. She had a sweet tooth so she made custards and chocolate puddings and she ate much too much of them. "Hurry, Herb, hurry. I feel faint. I'm nauseous. My feet are on fire. Herb . . ."

Villon recognized the sounds. The phone dropping, Lisa slumping to the floor. There was no time to call Arnold. He summoned one of his detectives and drove like a demon to what he prayed would be Lisa's rescue. They used a skeleton key to enter her apartment and found her prone on the floor. Villon picked her up in his arms and directed his detective to bring the milk bottle with them. They rushed Lisa to a hospital emergency room, where Villon identified himself and told the examining doctor he suspected Lisa had been poisoned with thallium nitrate. The doctor whistled, slightly off key, and had Lisa prepared for a stomach pumping. Her breathing had become unnatural and he feared for her life.

Villon sent the detective back to the precinct with the milk bottle, cursing the fool for not having held it with a handkerchief. He phoned the Garden of Allah but Arnold had left. Villon left messages for Arnold at his precinct and with Garbo in case Arnold phoned her.

Garbo paled when she heard of Lisa's condition.

"There's Gruber to worry about," said Villon. "You must get to him and caution him. And Greta, there's yourself."

"Well yes, but I only eat and drink what Lottie prepares for me. And I don't believe she is considering poisoning me. Are you, Lottie?"

Lottie smiled and continued with the tunafish salad she was preparing.

"I will alert Gruber," said Greta, and hung up. On the studio phone, she asked the operator to page Gruber, and then rescinded the request immediately. If they hear I am paging Gruber, they will suspect I'm up to something. The killer will guess that the poison has taken its effect on Lisa Schmidt. The killer. The poisoner. This madman, or is it a madwoman? There was a knock at the door and Lottie opened it. There stood Martin Gruber carrying a florist's box. Garbo didn't thank God, she thanked Guiss. "Come in, Martin. Lottie, shut the door. Put those foolish flowers aside." She told him about the attempt on Lisa's life. The bottles of milk.

"What are Lisa's chances?" Martin asked. He had fallen in love with her and only now that her life hung by a thread would he admit it to himself.

Garbo said, "Who would know where she lived?"

"Just about everyone connected with the production. There's always a list of personnel issued to everyone with addresses and phone numbers."

"And of course they would have access to it. Those monsters who are Guiss's associates. Martin, we are in terrible danger. You must be very careful."

"Don't worry about me. I will look after myself. I don't think they're on to me."

"Don't be so sure. They made much of a drama about the camera. Don't underestimate them. I have gotten to know them very well this past week. There isn't one of them who isn't capable of murder."

"I don't think it's Guiss. I have memorandums he has dictated about his displeasure at Hannah Baum and Kriegman's murders."

"I wonder if it's been noticed Lisa hasn't shown up for work. I have it! I will phone the lot and disguise my voice and say I am Lisa's girlfriend and she's been rushed to the hospital. A good idea, yes?" She was smart enough not to use the studio phone. She was connected to the set and gave an assistant the news. After which her face glowed and she said, "I'm a very good operative, aren't I? After all, I was an espionage agent in *Mysterious Lady,* and I was a pretty good Mata Hari, even if they had to hire June Knight to dance for me. Ha ha, how Marlene will be jealous when she hears about this!"

*   *   *

From FBI headquarters in downtown Los Angeles where he had been summoned for what proved to be a momentous meeting, Arnold Lake searched for Herb Villon by phone. He was directed to the hospital, where Herb told him Lisa Schmidt was putting up a tough struggle for survival. Villon had ordered additional protection for Garbo and assigned two detectives to go to the studio and bring in Martin Gruber for his own safety.

"I hope she pulls through, I'm crazy about her," Arnold said. Lisa might have been heartened by her burgeoning list of admirers. "Herb, I'm at headquarters. I've been there since early this morning. We got word the Germans are planning to call home a number of their agents, so we've got to move in on them and fast. We're closing the books today on Guiss and his bunch."

"This means shutting down the movie! What a blow that'll be to Greta and von Stroheim."

"Sorry, buddy. That's the toss of the dice."

"When does the operation begin?"

"It's underway at the castle right now."

Several weeks earlier, Agathe, who had posed as the Wolheim daughter and was now one of Risa Barron's maids, had found the courage to sneak out of the castle and turn herself in to Herb Villon. Herb and Arnold in turn convinced her she was more important to them at large in the castle than in custody.

"But I will be poisoned!" Agathe had protested tearfully.

Herb lied, "You could be executed as an enemy agent."

"Oh my God, wherever I turn lies death."

"You have nothing to fear in the castle. They won't kill anyone there. They don't want to give us an excuse to enter it. Be smart, Agathe, be as smart as they, say you've been in the dossier we have on you. . . ."

"Dossier." She repeated the word in a ghostly tone.

Arnold said smartly, "We're very big with dossiers. Go back to the castle. Watch what goes on carefully. Report to our boys who are inside."

"Boys? Inside?"

"Do you agree to go back?" persisted Villon.

Agathe said gravely, "How do they say it in England, 'In for a penny, in for a pound.' Okay. In espionage school they said I was the girl with the greatest potential. Well, I wasn't. I was no good as Fraulein Wolheim. Now I have an opportunity to redeem myself. You shall benefit from my training, ha. Ironic, isn't that so? Now, who are these boys inside?"

She was surprised and then delighted to be told that various gardeners, kitchen help, members of the swimming pool crew and the gardener who operated the lawn mower were all federal operatives who had carefully infiltrated Guiss's employ to prepare for his downfall.

"The man who runs the lawn mower? That's funny."

"What's so funny?" asked Herb.

"I have slept with him." She shrugged. "He's better with the lawn mower."

Villon phoned Garbo and told her Arnold's news. She exhaled, as though she'd been struck a blow in the stomach. Then just as quickly she said, "It's better this way. But Herbert, how will you know who is the poisoner? Will you ever find out who is Guiss's superior here in Los Angeles?" She thought for a moment and then said, "You know, I think I know who that might be. I shall confront this person."

That alarmed Villon. "Greta! Don't do anything foolish! You're no match for these people!"

"No match indeed! Haven't I outsmarted them! Haven't I outwitted them! I most certainly am their match!"

She didn't hear the door open. Lottie was clattering pots and pans in the kitchenette. He came in carrying an opened bottle of champagne. Then Greta saw his reflection in the dressing-room mirror, the bottle of champagne, and thought quickly and wisely. "Why how nice of you, Mr. Henkel. Champagne! And my favorite brand!"

"Don't drink it!" shouted Villon.

"Goodbye, Herb," she said sweetly. "Lottie, Gustav Henkel

brings me champagne. Gustav, it's so early in the morning for champagne. Wouldn't you prefer some of Lottie's exquisite hot chocolate?"

Henkel had been in his office when he heard Villon's two detectives arrive to take Martin Gruber into "custody." He knew then that time was running out and swiftly. He'd taken care of Lisa Schmidt, Martin Gruber would elude him, but there was Garbo, and she belonged to him. Her murder would give him immortality. He had a bottle of champagne laced with poison prepared for himself and the others. The authorities would never take him alive, he'd promised himself that a long time ago. He would be the savior of the others too. Lieb was a megalomaniac, and desperately in need of Henkel's help.

Guiss has been good to him. He'd spirited him out of Hamburg when the police were beginning to close in on him. Oh how he enjoyed killing people! It was wonderful to know they were dying in awful agony, with feet on fire and innards bursting with nausea and he was the master of their fates. Now it would soon be finished, but there was still much to accomplish. He went to Guiss's office with the bottle of champagne which contained more than enough thallium nitrate. He was killing Lisa Schmidt with small doses to prolong her agony; he had never liked her after she had unsubtly given him the name of a good local dentist.

Only Guiss was in the office. He was in a terrible state over Gruber's "arrest." Henkel sympathized. Guiss was busy emptying the files and desk drawers of what might be incriminating evidence. "Champagne? You choose now to drink champagne?"

"Why not?" said Henkel airily. "I've been saving this bottle for just such an occasion!" He brought two glasses from the bar, took them to the desk and filled them. "Come, Albert, this may be our last chance to drink together."

"I shouldn't drink with you at all. You murder Hannah Baum and Kriegman, and before Gruber was taken into custody, he told me Lisa Schmidt is in serious condition in the hospital. Oh Gustav, you have so much to account for. Where the hell is Werner? Where the hell is Risa? The fools."

"Come Albert, drink up." Henkel lifted his glass in a toast. "To absent friends!"

Guiss downed his in one gulp. Henkel refilled it. "It's very good stuff, Gustav. Did you bring it all the way from Hamburg?"

"No, it's from our cellar in the castle. Drink up."

Guiss said as he prepared to down the second glass with its lethal contents, "You know, I should have told you this a long time ago. But really, Gustav, you've got to do something about your teeth." He downed the glass and felt dizzy. He sank into his chair. "Gustav. Something's wrong with me. Do something. Call someone. I feel terrible. My feet are burning. This awful nausea . . . Oh Gustav! You rotten son of a bitch!"

The castle was taken over in an orderly fashion. The federal agents posing as employees knew who were German staff and who were innocents supplied by employment agencies. Werner Lieb had barricaded himself in his bedroom, where he disappointed Risa Barron by committing suicide with a bullet to his right temple. Risa Barron heard the shot, shook her head sadly, and wondered why Agathe, who was usually in a nervous and agitated state, stood so calmly at the window watching the federal agents leading their captives out of the castle into police wagons. Risa had her box of jewelry and a small suitcase. She planned on replenishing her lavish wardrobe at her next port of call. In a rare moment of kindness, she asked Agathe, "Look, do you want to come with me? To South America, to Rio? You can have a whole new life there."

"No," said Agathe. "But *bitte*. Thank you. I want to stay here in America. I think I will like it here."

Risa smiled. "You cooperated with them, didn't you?"

"To save my life, yes. I neutralized the electronic machinery. I had to sleep with the engineer to find out how, but he was pleasant. Are you sure you will escape them?"

Risa pressed a panel in a wall that revealed a hidden passage.

"Dear girl, I rented this place. And I chose this bedroom because of this hidden panel. The castle was built by a celebrated and delightfully perverted silent screen director. This is how he sneaked his girlfriends in from the outside under his wife's unsuspecting nose. Good luck to you, Agathe. Perhaps we will meet again." She hurried into the hidden passage and into the arms of a federal agent who had discovered the entrance to the passage in the gazebo in the garden.

"You do not drink the champagne, Greta?"

"It's too early for me. I told you that." She was sure Villon was on his way. Lottie came out of the kitchenette with two steaming cups of hot chocolate.

Lottie said to Greta, "Don't you dare drink that champagne. This morning they burn you at the stake. You must have a clear head. You must remember your cues for the fire. It can be very dangerous. I don't care how much precautions they said they've taken. Accidents can happen. Here Mr. Henkel, forget the champagne. I'll see to it that she drinks it after the scene is shot. Here," she said jovially, "join Miss Garbo in my special hot chocolate." She waved a cup under his nose. "Isn't that tempting?"

"Oh yes. Very tempting." He took the cup from her. Lottie took the bottle of champagne to the kitchenette. Henkel watched Garbo sip her hot chocolate and close her eyes in ecstacy. He drank some of his. It was truly delicious. He said to Garbo, "The police have arrested Martin Gruber." She said nothing. He drank more hot chocolate. "You're not surprised. You knew all about us. You led Albert on. You made him believe you loved him, that you wanted to come to Germany after the war." He drank again. "You were very clever, Greta. Did you guess I was the Hamburg poisoner?"

"Actually, I suspected Werner Lieb. He went to school in Hamburg. Guiss knew you murdered the Wolheims?"

"Yes."

"He protected you. Why? He was against the murders."

He chuckled and he drank more hot chocolate. Lottie was returning from the kitchen with a jug in her hand. "We are brothers. We loved each other." He grinned and the teeth looked more repulsive than ever. He held his cup out to Lottie. "You're anxious for me to enjoy more hot chocolate. It's so hot, like my feet. I know what you're doing to me." He winked at Lottie. "I know about your past, Lottie Lynton. We did a complete check on you. Isn't thallium nitrate wonderful?"

Lottie said matter-of-factly as she refilled his cup, "Sometimes it is and sometimes it ain't. When I tried it out on a horse, it worked real fast. She was an old nag and we had her in the barn behind the house. She pulled my husband's wagon. He was a junk dealer. He was planning to get rid of the animal anyway, she was old and near blind."

Garbo covered her mouth with a hand. Henkel was in the throes of agony, but she admired the way he never spilled a drop of the liquid, never took his eyes from Lottie's face.

"But Henry took forever," Lottie said, admiring her fingernails. "He had the constitution of an ox. He was over two hundred and fifty pounds and it was solid muscle. It seemed to take forever for him to die. Let me have the cup. It's beginning to spill." She saw the look of horror on Garbo's face. She was paralyzed by the sight of the dying man.

Henkel clutched his stomach. His eyes were on Garbo. Poor bitch. She has no stomach for this. She should have seen what Hannah Baum and Kriegman went through before they gave up the ghost. My feet, my feet, oh dear God in heaven, my feet. So this is what it's like? How could I. What a beast I am. He blurted, "Albert is dead. He drank the champagne. She would have had him killed anyway. He would not have survived. She ordered me to kill Hannah and Kriegman. She had a list and she was determined to wipe them all out. The Schmidt woman, Gruber and you, Greta Garbo, she despised you . . . oh my God . . . oh my God . . . despite her power in the Nazi party . . . she wanted to be *you*. . . ." He looked into Lottie's eyes. *"Danke."*

"Bitte," rejoindered Lottie as she watched him sink onto the floor.

Villon came rushing into the dressing room followed by Arnold, Villon shouting Greta's name.

Garbo was on her feet. "I'm all right. I'm fine. Lottie has the bottle of champagne." She pointed to Henkel's body. "He told me everything. There he is, chaps, the stiff. Do you know, he was Albert's brother? And there is a person who was more powerful than Albert."

"We know," said Arnold. "His wife. His widow."

The pyre was piled in the center of the sound stage. The outdoor set reminded Peter Lorre of the early impressionistic silent German films. It had the feel of *Caligari* and *Warning Shadows* and, for a while, Lorre was struck with a nostalgia for his homeland. Perhaps after the war. . . . His thoughts were interrupted by the entrance of Garbo with Villon and Arnold. There were over two hundred extras present. The actors impersonating the inquisitors were mostly impatient. Boris Karloff chafed at the heat of the lights needed for Technicolor shooting. Bela Lugosi, not needed in this sequence, came to see how von Stroheim would handle the burning. Von Stroheim was fussing with Alysia Hoffman, who looked stunning as the haughty noblewoman he had her portraying. She watched Garbo arriving. She saw Villon and Arnold. She grabbed one of von Stroheim's wrists and held it tightly.

"What's the matter with you, Alysia?"

"It's warm. Is my makeup running?"

"You look terrific. I'm going to shoot your big close-up before I set fire to Joan. Then I'll repeat it with the flames flickering on your face. The critics will praise that, take it from me. What's the matter with you? Why are you trembling? Oh it's you, Greta. I didn't send for you. I won't need you for at least another hour."

"You are wrong, Erich, I am needed now. You know Mr. Villon and Mr. Lake. They have come with very sad news. Erich, I'm sorry to have to tell you this, but there will be no *Joan the Magnificent.*"

Von Stroheim saw Sam Goldwyn and Sophie Gang materializing. Goldwyn had just learned that his studio had been overrun by an enemy spy ring, and almost suffered a stroke. Sophie Gang had calmed him with a stiff hooker of brandy after he demanded the spies be "determinated."

"Exterminated," Sophie corrected him.

Greta wanted to throw her arms around von Stroheim and comfort him. He was in a state of shock; his private world had collapsed. Goldwyn astonished her when he came forward and said, "I'm going to take over. I've been watching the rushes. I think they're mostly magnificent. Here and there a little too fussy, a little too fancy shmancy," he said, putting his arm around von Stroheim, "and we'll have a lot of disagreements, just like in the old days, okay Erich?"

Von Stroheim was so overcome with emotion, he struggled for words. "Sam, Sam, I . . . I love you Sam . . ."

"Careful!" cautioned Goldwyn, "there will be gossip. Better Greta should love me. At last we're working together. Where is she? Where did she go?"

Garbo was talking to Alysia Hoffman, who was surrounded on each side by Villon and Arnold. Alysia stood regally, hands at her sides, fists clenched, a look of pure arrogance and defiance on her face. "And I'm sorry to be the one to tell you, Albert is dead. His brother poisoned him."

Alysia's voice was shrill. "So? So? So now you know everything, *hein?* I suppose now I am to be taken into custody, ha! What a laugh." She said with a sneer, "For years I traveled Europe's capitols setting up the powerful structure of Albert Guiss. Guiss! Ha! He was Reinhold Henkel when I chose him to become the richest man in the world. Goering didn't like that but I have more power than that obese pig, more power than that odious cripple Goebbels; there are times when even Hitler fears me. And you, Greta Garbo, I molded you and your friend Mercedes like putty. You played into my hands so easily!"

Von Stroheim said to Goldwyn, "We may have to reshoot all of her scenes. How can we release a movie starring a master spy?"

Goldwyn was elated. "Are you mad? The publicity will be sensational. *Life* and *Look* and all the other magazines will fight for an exclusive. And I'll give it to all of them."

"But I need the close-ups I was going to do today! Now I won't be able to get them."

Goldwyn patted von Stroheim's shoulder. "Oh no? Just leave it to Irving."

"Your name is Sam, Mr. Goldwyn," Sophie Gang reminded him, eternal suffering etched in her face.

"I know my name, you silly woman."

Garbo studied Alysia's face as Goldwyn approached Arnold Lake. The woman's lips were working, but no sounds emerged. Her eyes were blinking wildly and for no reason whatsoever, she was fussing with her elaborate coiffure. Garbo moved back and took Villon's hand. It sent a tingle throughout his body. "Herb, Herb, look at her. Look at Alysia Hoffman. I think she's breaking down. She's going mad."

Alysia Hoffman began walking slowly toward von Stroheim. She looked around at her audience. The set had gone quite still. Someone was laughing maniacally. She didn't realize it was herself. And then she spoke in a voice underlined by hysteria. "I'm ready for my close-up, Mr. von Stroheim!"

Epilogue

The media went wild with the story of the cracking of Alysia Hoffman's spy ring. There was heavy speculation as to who else in the country might be working for the enemy. Risa Barron, in return for a promise of sympathetic treatment, gave the FBI an extensive list of traitors in their midst. There was quite a fuss over the confiscation of her fabulous jewel collection, Risa storming, "Damn you! I worked like hell for them." She wasn't doubted, but they were held in custody until after the war, when a shrewd Jewish lawyer won her her freedom and the return of her property, and she fled to Brazil, where she opened a chain of jewelry stores.

After *Joan the Magnificent* was completed, Greta Garbo left Hollywood, little realizing she would never make another film. She did do a test for a projected Walter Wanger production years later and there was talk she would accept a cameo role in a possible filming of Proust's *Remembrance of Things Past,* but instead she traveled the world like the Flying Dutchman, doomed to keep on the go, until finally she settled into an apartment in New York City.

While *Joan* was still shooting, Garbo stayed in touch with Villon and Arnold. They were good friends now, and although she had every reason to believe Herb Villon was hopelessly in love with her, she did nothing to encourage him. Strangely enough, while work continued on *Joan,* there was no longer a fire or a passion in either Garbo's work or von Stroheim's direction. He would admit to no one how deeply he had become committed to Alysia Hoffman, and he seemed listless and unhappy.

Mercedes de Acosta wrote a sizzling autobiography, *Here Lies the Heart,* published in 1960 by Reynal, in which she shamelessly and sizzlingly claimed or implied lesbian relationships with not only Garbo, but also Dietrich, Claudette Colbert and Eva Le Gallienne, to name just a chosen few. There were some eye-popping photos to illustrate her allegations, including several of Garbo nude on an isolated island.

Salka Viertel retired to Switzerland. Her son Peter, who had worked on the screenplay of *The African Queen,* wrote a book about John Huston and the filming, *White Hunter, Black Heart,* which in turn was eventually filmed by Clint Eastwood, who directed and impersonated Huston. Peter had the good taste to marry Deborah Kerr.

Peter Lorre and Bela Lugosi died of their drug addictions, in the later stages of their lives reduced to appearing in cheap quickies. They were almost unrecognizable.

Von Stroheim returned to acting, featured mostly as nasty Germans until the war ended. He returned to Europe, where he continued acting, mostly in France, and then in 1950 Billy Wilder brought him back to Hollywood to co-star in Gloria Swanson's brilliant comeback film, *Sunset Boulevard.* The film did little to revive their careers.

William Haines was arrested after the war on charges of impairing the morals of a minor. He escaped a jail sentence but his life was ruined. Six months after his death, his grief-stricken lover committed suicide.

Agathe, whose last name was Schulman, sold her memoirs of her life as a spy to an eager publisher in New York. It sold well and was the basis of a successful television series. The book was pure fabrication, but it made Agathe wealthy and she married a Mexican playboy who beat her regularly and succeeded in divesting her of most of her savings.

Marion Davies never succeeded in buying the house which was the scene of two murders. Shortly after the war, Hearst was on the verge of bankruptcy and in danger of losing his vast newspaper empire. Marion, gallant and loyal to the very end, handed him a paper bag filled with her jewel collection, the sight of which would have caused Risa Barron to hemorrhage, and Hearst was rescued.

Arnold Lake returned to Washington, D.C., married a dried-out debutante, and tried to run for office as president of the United States. He did not succeed and returned to his law practice and sired three sons, all redneck anti-Semites. He continued to send Christmas cards to Herb Villon.

Hazel Dickson returned from the war a changed woman. Herb Villon expected to marry her, but she was having none of it. A former gossip columnist for a newspaper syndicate, she moved from gossip writing to political analyzing and became a terror in print. Herb never married. He retired to Las Vegas and, until her death, kept in touch with Garbo.

Before Billy Haines's death and her permanent move to New York, Garbo invited him to the Beverly Hills hotel where she was temporarily in residence, to have lunch with her. When he arrived, she realized he wasn't the same Billy Haines she used to know.

"You are so sad, Billy. Why don't you come to New York with me? There is no Hollywood any more. Here, you are a dinosaur."

"Worse. I'm a leper. I can't even cry on Crawford's shoulder. She's moved to New York. Oh what the hell. I've got a house, I've got money, I'll just be that perverted old man on the hill. By the way, whatever became of *Joan the Magnificent?*"

Garbo stroked her chin. "I'm not quite sure. Goldwyn said it was too terrible to release, so now it sits somewhere in storage, unwanted, unloved, like me."

"Albert Guiss loved you."

"Yes, he really did. Very tragic. He could have been a great man, but he ran with the wrong crowd." She laughed. "You know, I've never told this to anyone before. Billy," she leaned forward with a sly look, "I went to bed with him. Ha ha ha."

Haines raised an eyebrow. "So did I dearie, so did I!"

They enjoyed sharing a laugh after so much gloom. "You should have heard the comments of my beloved Lottie Lynton when she suspected I'd caved in to Albert's advances. Poor, dear Lottie."

"Say, whatever became of her?"

"Oh don't you know? She fell in love with a man who owned a service station in Pasadena. But very soon the marriage went sour and so you know what?"

"No. What?"

"He poisoned her! Ha Ha Ha Ha Ha!"